SIGHTS

Susanna Vance

Sights

DELACORTE PRESS

Published by
Delacorte Press
an imprint of Random House Children's Books
a division of Random House, Inc.
1540 Broadway
New York, New York 10036

Visit us on the Web! www.randomhouse.com/teens
Educators and librarians, for a variety of teaching tools,
visit us at www.randomhouse.com/teachers

Library of Congress Cataloging-in-Publication Data

Vance, Susanna.
   Sights / Susanna Vance.
      p. cm.
   Summary: Despite years of abuse at the hands of her drunken father,
Baby Girl has always believed that she was special, partly because of her "gift"
of seeing the future, until she and her mother set out to begin a new life on
their own.
   ISBN 0-385-32761-7
   [1. Mothers and daughters–Fiction. 2. Self-perception–Fiction. 3. High
schools–Fiction. 4. Schools–Fiction. 5. Child abuse–Fiction.] I. Title.

PZ7.V2767 Si 2001
[Fic]–dc21

                                                                    00-035826

The text of this book is set in 11.5-point Berthold Garamond.
Book design by Debora Smith

Manufactured in the United States of America
March 2001
10 9 8 7 6 5 4 3 2 1
BVG

For Donald B. Wright
my husband, my sweetheart, my buddy

Special thanks to

my editor,
Diana Capriotti,
whose steadying hand is evident
on every page

and my sister,
Ingrid V. Aubry,
who is with me
book to book, cover to cover

CHAPTER 1

Born Special

I was in the womb eleven and one half months, came out fat, durable and gorgeous. I've seen the newborn pictures: smooth broad ears, a few sharp little teeth glinting like Chiclets. It wasn't that I was overdue, it just took extra time for me to get ready. I have no way of knowing how ordinary babies do it, but when I was ready, I came out.

It was an animal doctor who delivered me. My father arranged it in a bargain struck with the local vet. Dad ran a pick-up service, cleaning out veterinarians' animal incinerators, selling the leavings to an outfit that bagged them as a tonic for garden dirt. HAUL YOUR ASHES is what it said on the sides of our special coupe. That '45 Chevy was my dad's pride and joy. Only two years old and black as the ace of spades. He'd taken the car's backseat out and broken through to the trunk, giving him room for all the ashes in the world.

When I was born I screamed for a while, I couldn't help it, my head hurt like Hades. My first sight in broad daylight was the vet's sweaty face, quivering from the effort of getting me out. He held me away from him like I was rabies.

"Man alive," he muttered, prodding at my solid haunch. "Same gestation as a walrus."

I heard him and he knew it.

If I reminded him of a walrus, I came by it naturally. My dad was a dead ringer for one: sleek-dark and heavy, with a mustache like oiled bristle.

Dad and the vet allowed I looked like my mother, Bettina, a blond beauty. The difference being I was strapping large and she was petite.

". . . So purdy . . . ," Momma said faintly, hardly even alive from what she'd been through.

"So!" the vet said. "Whatcha naming her?"

"Baby Girl." Voice weaker by the minute. "She's my baby girl—"

Dad snorted. "That's the stupidest name that ever lived. The kid's already *big*—you think she's not going to get *bigger*? That folks won't laugh at her being called *Baby Girl*?"

I looked from one parent to the other. I thought Baby Girl was real to the point and showed how it would be between me and my mother.

Momma was past answering. Her eyes wandered fuzzily around at the roomful of cages. Cats and dogs pressed

2

their noses to the wire and looked back at us with scandalized faces.

Now that I'm old enough to know such things, Momma's told me the story. "It all came as a surprise, Baby Girl. What happened that day."

I'd been inside her so long, she'd started thinking that was just how it was. The last thing she imagined was me being born on a cold steel table meant for examining collie dogs.

She and Dad had been sitting in a theater, watching a movie with the latest blond actress, Marilyn Monroe. Dad saying all the way through, *Man alive, I'm gonna hop a bus to Hollywood, get that bombshell's number!* This made Momma, who was just as much a bombshell, not feel too swell about how she looked.

The audience started in clapping and hooting at something Miss Monroe was doing. When I heard the whistles—being an innocent unborn—I figured it was all for me and decided this was the moment to come out.

Momma got my signal and quick pulled Dad up the aisle. Once they were in the car, he amazed her by driving right by the hospital. Instead, he turned in at the Paw and Claw Clinic and herded her in its back door. She didn't know one thing about the arrangement! But by then, the crowning of my head was cleaving her like a chain saw and there wasn't much she could do about it.

"The best things in life come with pain, Baby Girl," is what she says now. "I guess that makes you my very best thing."

For years she walked with a pitiful limp, the direct up-shot of me being born.

And worse, she didn't lose that unfocused look until I was thirteen and her eyes flew open to the truth.

Up till then, she just wouldn't face facts.

"I don't know what your dad was *thinking,* Baby Girl, taking us in there with Siamese cats." She pondered this notion as she hung out Dad's clothes, fried up his pork chops, scrubbed the ashes from his overalls. "It's just not like your dad to do such a thing."

It was completely like him. I saw that from the begin-ning.

If Momma had been thinking straight, she'd have seen it too. And seen that she was actually lucky we'd had no more than a vet. A real doctor would have kept tabs on her, not let me stay inside her all that time.

It was the staying inside that made me special.

Inside is where I got the Sight.

CHAPTER 2

---◉---

Between Him and Me

I remember how it was inside the womb. Although now that I'm older, I doubt there really were lace curtains or a canopy bed. The more important features, I am sure of.

I'd been developing for about ten months and had just started cutting my first teeth when suddenly my eyes focused beyond the close darkness of the womb. My special mind zoomed around in a universe where, instead of moons and stars, there were words and pictures of the future. I didn't know anything yet—I wasn't even born—but here I was beholding the wag of poodle tails and the flap of a moldy-winged parrot. Later, of course, once I was born into the vet's back room, I saw these creatures again for real.

There came more: images of a mother, blond and sweet

as taffy; 'venging angels, swording down the wicked—and pompoms that went *stitt stitt stitt* in my face like flocks of paper serpents.

It was the Sight I had, all right.

After I became a toddler and learned to speak, Momma knew I had it too. She said there were lots of names for my condition, but call it what you want, they all meant seeing into the future.

She'd had a great-aunt Lubmilla, who, like all my mother's kin, lived and died in the country of Latvia. Aunt Lubmilla also'd had a mild case of the Sight.

I sat propped in one corner of the built-in sofa, listening to Momma and nodding at the pictures that flooded my head.

I spoke in my perfect clear little voice: "Aunt Vanilla went boom?"

"Why, yes, sweetheart! Bombed to smithereens in the war." Momma smoothed my ringlets. "Leave it to you to know."

Dad looked up from the eating nook, where he polished his silver deer-killing bullets, and said, "Puhh!"

But Momma had proof of Aunt Lubmilla's powers, in the form of a fringed pillow somehow passed down from her to us. It was always kept smack in the center of our sofa. It smelled like unwashed parsnips, and the layered embroidery was shadow-deep and the color of forests. On it she'd stitched a darkish skin-and-bones angel, surrounded by a border of swords and knives. The angel was more like an insect-person, from the look of her bulging yellow eyes and her skimpy, threadbare wings. Her wide lips were open and a bobbly string of foreign words was stitched there, like she was speaking.

"It's a foretelling," Momma said. She stroked the fringe as she translated. " 'Soon, flying through the air, fewer angels, more regular peoples.' "

This didn't make a lick of sense to me, but Momma said it was now a scientific fact. Our aunt Lubmilla somehow knew about airplanes ahead of time.

Dad scowled at me and Momma sitting there, so raptured with each other.

"Bettina?" he said. "You wouldn't know a scientific fact if it bit you on your rosy butt."

Momma set the pillow down real quiet.

As far back as then, I knew our trailer was like a teetery canoe: Dad at one end, me at the other, Momma standing square in the middle, balancing it. She'd learned to hardly breathe, for fear of tipping us over.

From the minute I was born, I was crazy about Momma. But when she gave me her bosom, she like to smothered me. I still can't abide having things pushed in my face. My dad can vouch for that.

Once we got settled in at home, he got in the habit of jamming his thumb in my mouth. As if I'd want to suck that salty rough thing! I swiveled my head this way and that, but he kept poking it in. Then it came over me that I was a special baby, born with sharp little teeth, so I grabbed on to his thumb like a born bulldog and bit till I came to the bone.

7

He held my nose until I turned blue, but I didn't turn him loose till I died.

My momma worked air back into my lungs and I started back up again. I didn't cry, but she sure did.

It shocked Dad that a baby girl, something he expected to be as docile as my mother, could get the best of him. He drove to the vet, who refused to give him a tetanus shot or stitch him up, on account of the true rumor that Dad had gone and bought his own crematorium and was roasting down neighbor dogs and stray cats for extra bone ash profits.

Dad kicked over the vet's waiting room aquarium. Fish flipped around in puddles of broken glass, stretching open their mouths like they were trying to scream. For the next ten years, Dad would over and over recount the details to Mom and me.

The fish didn't make any noise, but the receptionist did. She was frantic, plucking up the fish, dropping them in her glass of Coca-Cola, the only liquid I guess she had on hand. Dad always cracked himself up at this part in the story.

"Something 'bout Coke-Cola kills fish dead as doorknobs. . . ." He'd be laughing so hard, the words came out as sobs. "Don't you get it? It was that screaming girl killed them goldfish 'stead of me! Bettina? How's that not funny? I swear half the girls on this planet is born lackin' a funny bone."

Next, as Dad continues the story, the vet cried out, "Are you *crazy?*" Dad raised his fist to him. "You are! You're *crazy!*"

"Call it what you want, Doc—someone crosses me, they *pay.*" Dad snagged a leather muzzle on his way out the door. "They pay through the *nose.*"

Get it? Dad would ask Mom. *Nose? Muzzle?*

He bragged how he came home proud as a peacock that day, strapped the muzzle onto my face. Nodded in satisfaction. "That'll fix your wagon."

Momma had jumped up and taken the muzzle straight off me again.

After I bit Dad, he just quit fooling with me, never picked me up again. It was over between us before it even started.

Our landlady lived on a steep rise above us. Her house was a freckled-brick ranch-style mansion with a fully attached three-car garage and painted white rocks along the concrete drive. Our trailer had a big dent in its top, which made me think it somehow fell off her hill, landed upside down and rolled back upright. I imagined it being too much trouble for her to haul back up, so she rented it out.

The landlady had permed gray hair, thick ankles and a speedy voice. She liked me and Momma, but she did not like my father. She said he was a lie-about and a bully. My dad said she was a buttinski and a jumper-to-conclusions.

Momma had to agree about her jumping to conclusions. One time the power went out and she drove top-speed all the way to church, waiting for the Apocalypse to hit. Another time she saw a mild-faced man in a cowboy hat buying a box of Post Toasties. Took him for Gene

Autry. He denied any knowledge of Hollywood or tumbleweeds, but she got his autograph on an Ivory Snow coupon and framed it for over her mantel. *Lester Jake Fishburn* is what it says.

She wasn't one for checking into things, but she always made me and Momma welcome.

Momma showed her gratefulness for the landlady's care by giving her home perms and sewing her up fancy little accessories on the Singer. Momma was a whiz on her Singer.

Those are my first recollections: the incident with Dad's thick hairy thumb, what he said to Momma when she was explaining Aunt Lubmilla's pillow, and how the landlady didn't like him. After that, I don't have another strong memory till I was three.

It's a bad one.

Dad scooped out a heaping tablespoon of SaniFlush, the white, grainy lye Momma used for cleaning the toilet.

"Open your trap," he said.

I wouldn't.

He took a nicer tone. "It's pure sweet sugar. C'mon . . . Daddy's little piggy loves sug-sug-sugar. . . ."

I *am* known to have a fondness for sugar.

My shrieks brought the landlady running down the bank. She took one look at me—foaming at the mouth—and said, "Oh Lord, she's a goner!"

Jumping to another conclusion.

The hospital gave me ether so they could fix my gullet

back up. That maskful of sleeping gas was worse than the poison, worse than death itself. It started an agony of smotheration and electrocuting visions.

Then I slid under and landed back in the womb, floating in fog and seawater, the future imprinted on my wide-open eyes. A shine came from inside me and lighted the way. It was my mother's future, but I was there. The only time I ever got a Sight of myself.

In it I was propped in deep blankets in the back of the Chevy, face pressed against a cold black pane of glass. Outside twisted the night highway, white slashes flicking down its center like sparks. A trafficless road, deep and lonesome as a gulch. Momma was at the wheel, our future unforeseeable beyond skewed headlights.

Dad told everyone I'd done it to myself. Swallowed lye to get attention. That it had cost him a fortune to fix me, just when he most couldn't afford it. The law had found his incinerator and a pile of strays, and shut him down. It was jail time or our savings. Momma told me later she voted for jail. It wasn't a long stretch, not in those days, but he wouldn't go. So, between the cost of the fine and the hospital, we were right down there. But Dad didn't poison me because he was mad about money or because of any other of his daily gripes. He poisoned me because he just wanted me dead. That's the way it was between him and me.

Momma had me recuperating on the cot in front of the space heater where she could keep an eye on me. I waited till she was in the kitchen dishing up sherbet to soothe my throat to give the news to Dad.

"I can read, Daddy," I croaked, my three-year-old voice permanently froggy from a scarred voice box.

"Ha. You got nine lives and you're hairy as a coconut, but you're no genius."

I was in no way as hairy as he was.

"It's the future I can read." I stared unblinking at him. "You aren't there, but I am."

He turned the dark ugly color of meat.

It was his way to do his worst to me when Momma was out of sight. Because we lived in a little trailer, it was another seven years before he got his big chance.

I was in fifth grade and the teacher's pet. She believed me to be a star: I was good in all subjects except math, could do four hundred sit-ups, and had girlfriends who fought to sit next to me.

My teacher told Momma I was well-rounded, and that my name was just plain original.

I came home from school one day happy as a bubble from winning another spelling bee. My friends Beverly and Penny and Madeline were only allowed to walk me as far as the landlady's house, on account of all the trouble my dad had been in.

They each had a different way of saying goodbye.

"*Adiós, muchacha!*" Beverly rattled the words to perfection. She was a brain and was teaching her own self Spanish.

"Praise the Lord!" Madeline cried. She was being raised by her grandma, and the two of them were dedicated to church. She's the one got me to knowing what a good baby Jesus had been, and how, like me, he'd gone on to be popular with 'most everyone.

"Y'ain't nothin' but a hound dog!" Penny called as I made my way down the embankment to our trailer. Penny and I were both one hundred percent nuts for Elvis Presley.

I called back, "See you laters, alligators!" A little joke we had.

I didn't have a clue what was about to happen.

I climbed the two steps to the trailer and stood on the little awning-covered stoop, listening through the bent aluminum door. Dad was yelling at Momma again, Momma making little murmurs but never speaking up. It was probably another rant about Momma refusing to let him do anything to her that would end her up giving birth on the vet's table again—a policy that hadn't done a thing to improve my dad's disposition.

Finally the back door slammed. Momma's way of solving things was to go hang wash out back, to calm her nerves.

Dad banged out the front. I knew he was headed off to do something bad to the vet again. Once you made it onto Dad's black list, he never gave up paying you back. Not ever.

I froze stiff, waiting for him to pass. He almost walked right by. But at the last second he punched his arm straight out from his side, bull's-eye, without even bothering to look. Knocked me straight out.

Momma found me down on the ground and managed to get me inside. I wouldn't wake up. Dad had taken the coupe so she got the landlady to drive us to the hospital again. I had a fractured cheekbone and a bruise to the brain. I stayed inside a coma for two days. Not only Sights but Sounds and Smells raced through my blood. Coming at me were people I didn't know, music I'd never heard, the mushed fragrance of fruits, heavy as fallen roses. Ball gowns waggled their petticoats at me and whirled around without any dancers inside. Nothing made sense, and I was real eager to get back out of myself and into waking life.

When I came to, Momma's face was bleary from crying. Dad sat in the only chair, pouting and staring out the hospital window.

"Oh, Baby Girl, you took such a bad fall I thought we were going to lose you." Momma dabbed her eyes. "You were *comatose*, precious lamb! But I knew you had the spirit to shake free."

It was hardly a fall I took, but Dad didn't say otherwise, and neither did I.

Afterward the landlady said, "I never knew a child to have so many accidents . . ."

It was a question, I knew that.

"My Baby Girl has a way of attracting trouble," Momma said, smiling down at me.

14

I stared back into her eyes. They were unseeing and untroubled as posies.

The landlady cocked her head at Momma too, knowing Momma never told lies. Finally she shook her head and mumbled, "That child's going to have to have enough sight for both of them . . . if she's going to stay alive."

Momma took her clucking for simple concern.

Me and Penny were ten when we started having weekly Elvis Presley Fan Club meetings. We did them over at her house. She lived in a trailer too, but hers was a big sunny type, lined up in a park with others like it. There were picket fences, shade trees and real paving. She was allowed to use her brother's Schwinn, and her dad was the milkman—even wore a uniform. She had it made.

In the wintertimes, we listened to Elvis records in her room, and if her mother wasn't home, we had screaming contests to prove our devotion to him. In summertimes, we held most of our club meetings riding around on the borrowed Schwinn.

I pedaled, on account of how my legs were meant for that sort of activity. I never got tired, even going uphill.

One spring day I remember real clear, because everything about it was so fun. Penny was sitting on the handlebars, curly red hair flipping me in the face, keeping me from seeing too good. She was wearing lipstick. She never got caught because the lipstick was white, and she was already naturally pale.

"Question Eighteen," she called over the wind of our speeding bicycle. "What is the color of Elvis's eyes?"

"Green."

"Hunh-unh. Blue."

"Okay, greenish blue. My turn. Question Nineteen: what was the name of Elvis's dead twin brother?"

We always sighed over that one. What if the little fellow'd made it? Me and Penny could each have had a true love of our own.

"Jessie Garon Presley. Of course."

I stood to pedal straight-legged. We were coming to the top of Drop-Off Hill. The timing was perfect for our most thrilling question.

Penny looked over her shoulder, eyes locked with mine. Her hands gripped the handlebars, turned white as her made-up lips.

"Question *Twenty*," I croaked. My eyes dimmed, the horizon replaced by the Technicolor, soft-lipped, dreamy-eyed face of Elvis. "In the movie, who was Elvis singing 'Love Me Tender' to?"

"*Meeee!*" we screamed together.

I lifted my feet from the pedals and we flew down the steep hill, heads back, hearts full to busting, screaming all the way to the bottom.

We were fans all right.

Me and Momma's best times were late evening. She let me stay up even on school nights. Dad had a whiskey habit, which began when he got up late in the morning and ended when he fell asleep early at night. He could only sleep in the closed-in slit of bed built into the back of the trailer. At least that's what he said whenever Momma brought up us maybe moving on. Moving up a little in the world.

"Leave it to you, Bettina, to act like I'm not a success in the small-business world. Trying to run me out of the one place I can sleep! Slumber's the only pleasure I get in bed, now you're so stingy with your precious thingamabob."

We could count on the strict hours Dad kept for passing out. Nine P.M. prompt, still clutching his whiskey bottle and a crumpled picture of Marilyn Monroe, he'd crawl into his box like an opposite-vampire—one who feared the night. Once the snoring started, nothing, not even the spin of our off-balance washing machine, could wake him before nine in the A.M.

Me and Momma could sing and dance loud as we wanted, and we did. With Dad hibernating, nighttime was always a party.

CHAPTER 3

Momma to the Rescue

That was my past, before I made it to the end of my thir-teenth year. Up till then, age thirteen had been a lucky number. It had meant starting junior high, which was even better than Momma said it would be.

We had six different classes with six different subjects. Homeroom was the most important. Your first-period teacher was your homeroom teacher. She kept a special eye on you and was in charge of handing out advice.

I was doing good in almost everything. The exception being multiplication tables. Me and Momma were working on that in the evenings, using flash cards. Of course my dad thought that my being slow at numbers was one more defect.

If I ever started to believe my dad's low opinion of me,

my friend Beverly would chime in to make me feel better. "You're perfect, Baby Girl," she'd say, in that pleasant light-toned voice of hers. Having nothing much left of a voice myself, I always notice that in others. "Everyone likes your big pink cheeks. Who cares about seven times nine?"

I had to agree.

One day, the four of us friends were sprawled on the sidewalk in front of school, playing jacks. I was snatching them up like I couldn't go wrong. Three bounces of the ball, three jacks in my hand—and two of them kissies!

Madeline complimented my moves with a hallelujah.

When the ball hit a crack and I missed picking up the last of my sixies, Penny, who like me was still a lot more interested in Elvis than Jesus, said, "No fault of yours, Baby Girl, just bum luck that ball went stray."

I shrugged. "I knew it was going to happen."

"It is *so cool*," Beverly said, "having a friend with the Sight." She blew me a kiss.

Last year I foretold that Bev's poor parakeet would likely get eaten by the neighbor dog. When the Fuller Brush man let it fly out their front door, my warning had her ready. She leaped the fence and snatched it right back out of Duke's mouth.

Since that day, she like to worshipped me.

"Yea and verily." Madeline nodded, rhinestone cross twinkling between the edges of her Peter Pan collar. "You have a gift from on high."

We smiled at each other.

We were looking forward to ninth grade. Our final year in junior high. Top dogs at last! I'd be eligible to play A-team volleyball and expected I'd make it to the state spelling bee.

Already, I had so many after-school activities I was hardly home when my dad wasn't asleep, or Momma there to guard me. It seemed like Dad wasn't even a danger anymore.

Then came the picnic at Slippery Creek.

Momma packed all Dad's favorites for the outing: Vienna Sausages, Ritz Crackers, Cheez Whiz, beer. Dad and I ate everything. He laid there on the blanket, grinding his tusky teeth, swallowing a dozen greasy little sausages at a time. Pat-patting his big hard stomach. I pictured flippers and the gulping of whole fish. Whole children!

I was parched from all the Ritzes. I reached for my bottle of Orange Crush, but suddenly Dad had it and was turning it upside down. My mouth puckered, watching it leak into the stony ground.

Momma had gone back to the car for the transistor radio and a bag of marshmallows.

Dad handed me his cold can of Blue Collar.

"Go on," he said. "Toss it back," grinning like we were buddies.

I wanted to believe he'd turned nice. The beer was so cold and relaxing. While Momma wasn't looking, I chugged down quite a bit. Dad popped open another.

We dillydallied like that, watching Momma work her heinie off. She gathered twigs to roast marshmallows, washed our plates, chased off ants and yellow jackets. The little plastic radio was playing "Ain't Got a Barrel of Money," and Momma sang along in the same clear high voice I think I would have had, if you-know-who hadn't done you-know-what to me.

Then she headed up the hill and disappeared into the woods to pee.

That was the moment Dad jumped up and said I should go play in the creek. In fact, when I was slow about it, he shoved me right in.

I was so dizzy from the beer, I slipped on the mossy rocks and went over a steep underwater ledge. That quick I was on the deep creek bottom, drowning.

Dad sat down to watch. Even through the gurgle of water, I swear I could hear him singsonging, "That'll fix her wagon, fix her wagon, fix . . ."

Momma came plowing down the hill, pedal pushers flapping open at the waist. Even as I thrashed in the water, I was aware she'd finally witnessed the truth between me and Dad. She threw herself in the creek. The sound of her little feet eggbeatering through the water thrilled me to the quick. My Sight rose up and I saw she was a hero—remembered the vision of our life through a car window. This kept me hanging on till she could grab my head and haul me out.

After she saw I was still ticking, she zipped up her dripping pants and punched my Dad in the neck, causing a divorce.

When we all got back home, Momma's forehead was still in a frown, her eyes for the first time in bright, beaming focus. She scrubbed the Chevy inside out, rinsing away old ashes till her bucket of Pine Sol went thick and gray with the ghosts of unfortunate animals.

Dad chewed his mustache, peeking out the trailer window, maybe thinking she was trying to make up for socking him and how at some point he'd forgive her because it was me who caused the whole problem anyway, and where would he find another wife half so pretty as the one he had?

That night Momma came to my bed. The bug light outside my window showed the fine shape of her cheek and a mouth shapely and pink as a movie star's.

She whispered, "It's not your fault, Baby Girl, your dad just don't like you and now I got to choose."

I never doubted she'd choose right.

We both knew he'd kill us if he saw us going. He would specially kill us if he knew we were taking his precious '45 Chevy, even though it was fifteen years old—now older than me!—and round in all the places cars had grown sharp and stylish. This meant sneaking out of the trailer while he sawed logs. We lugged Momma's Singer Slant Needle between us and quick loaded our things into the back of the pine-smelling Chevy. We piled soft old coverlets and pillows in there so we could go anywhere we wanted and have a handy place to sleep.

As we pulled away, Momma flicked on the headlights and honked the horn. We burst out laughing. There was no chance in the world that he heard us, no chance in the world he'd come after us. For one thing, we had the car! Plus he was tied to that trailer: the ratty bed, his reeking bottle of whiskey, that faded Marilyn Monroe picture.

He'd never leave. This was *sayonara.*

We sped down the highway toward midnight, putting hours between us and the trailer. I was burrowed into the back of the Chevy, head deep in Aunt Lubmilla's earth-smelling pillow, watching telephone poles race by. Momma'd brought her dress forms, which were nice company even though they were headless. But the more I tried to sleep, the more I got the jimmies.

"Momma?" I called to the back of her head. "Why's Aunt Lubmilla's pillow have all those knives on it? I thought angels were mild-natured, just flew around drinking pollen and whatnot."

"No, honey, you're getting confused with butterflies. Those old-time angels were strictly eye-for-an-eye. Lubmilla probably meant those to be swords of vengeance."

"Oh."

That gave me something to think about, angels slicing up their enemies. But it didn't do a thing to help me sleep.

"Momma? How'd you get started up with Dad?"

"Well, honey, I was real young. He had a powerful-strong way about him . . . a fine powerful-strong build. . . ."

"Oh." I sat up and hooked my chin over the back of Momma's seat, but nothing more was coming.

Warm night-smelling air poured through her side vent. I watched the gruesome rain of millers spackle the windshield. Floating on the underside of the glass was my own distorted reflection: a wide gray mushroom of a sad face.

Heartsickness swamped me.

"Momma?" My voice snagged on the velvet breeze. "I guess I'll never be seeing my friends again? Talk Jesus with Madeline or share my feelings for Elvis with Penny . . . ?"

"Oh, Baby Girl." She gave her head a tiny shake. "I'm real sorry you had to leave your fine friends behind. . . . I promise we'll find us a good place . . . more friends will come."

"I got you, Momma." I sniffed a little. "That's enough for me."

We took the next corner and were about blinded by the loud red and yellow lights of a truck stop. Momma swung the car into its parking lot, spewing gravel as she braked. "How 'bout we cheer up with a little bite of something?"

I smiled. "Okay."

We batted our way through crusty June bugs trying to get in the door with us. It was something, going to a restaurant in the middle of the night! We ordered doughnuts and coffee. My first coffee, heavy with cream and sugar.

"Nothin's going to stunt your growth, Baby Girl," Momma said. Then as an afterthought, "But swear you won't take to smoking right off."

I swore. Anything my dad did, I didn't want to do.

I smacked down the last grains of coffee-sugar and we walked out feeling ready for anything.

Momma popped the glove compartment and pulled out

a pint of shiny gold paint and two narrow brushes. Right then and there, we painted big gold flowers over the words HAUL YOUR ASHES. She'd thought of everything.

Our new life already suited me better than the one back at the trailer.

It was springtime when we drove away from our past, so I hardly missed a lick of school. It took a lot of driving before our nerves settled, but we were soon calm as cucumbers, happy to be anywhere but home.

There wasn't anything me and Momma didn't talk about, having all that time in the car. She sang along with the radio, which I loved even though it wasn't something I could do myself. We did multiplication tables. I stared at passing scenery.

I also stared at Momma herself. From back in my padded sleeping chamber, I watched her in the rearview mirror, her newly capable eyes a joy to me. When I sat up front, I watched her looking between the spokes of the steering wheel, concentrating on the road. Marveled at the smooth sure flex of her legs, her patent leather pumps clutching, braking, tapping on the brights.

I noticed again how me and Momma looked alike. We had the same blond skin and hair. Fair coloring that came from Latvia. Me and Momma and Aunt Lubmilla all had Lettish blood, is how Momma explained it. Making it sound like we were part salad.

Of course we didn't look *exactly* alike. The differences showed in my thick arms and legs, coated in hair that was luckily a pale color—peach fuzz Momma called it—and an unblinking face. Things that came from the Walrus side of the family.

Still, I saw the two of us as a matched set of dolls, every day wearing the wardrobe of twin clothes Momma had sewed up for us.

I was maybe too old for this, but Momma and me were particular close. Everyone said that. Specially my friend Madeline, who loved her grandma but prayed every night for a young pretty mom like mine. I guess I wouldn't be seeing much of old Madeline anymore. Or Penny. Or Beverly . . .

Whenever tears came up my throat, I swallowed them back down with animal crackers and Orange Crush.

I didn't notice Momma having any struggle with tears. Every mile we put between us and Dad seemed to give her more confidence. She spoke right up if the service station boy forgot to check the oil or left soapy streaks on the glass. She even lost the limp she'd had since I was born. Her take-charge attitude was promising to last!

When a bank manager gave her a little stack of cash for the savings book she'd brought along, she laughed right out loud. We started using motels every few days after that, where we'd spend most our time taking showers.

The money took us through two months and nine states before we started getting low on cash. Momma and I figured out a plan where I could use my Sight as a way to keep us going. Dazzle people for free gallons of gas or Breakfast Specials.

"Do you mind, Baby Girl?" She worried the steering wheel. "Once we get settled, we got the Singer to see us through."

"I do not mind one whit, Momma."

In fact I really took to the idea of being able to help out. As it turned out, though, I didn't have to do it but once.

CHAPTER 4

———◉———

Going into Business

First place we came to, after we'd agreed on our new way of getting what we needed, was the town of Cot.

Customers gawked as we came in the diner wearing our twin mint-green puffed-sleeve dresses, our matching small and medium white plastic purses clutched just so. We knew from the miles of orchards we'd passed that this was a town of apricot farmers, who were maybe not that accustomed to female beauty. Momma had applied rouge to our cheeks in the Chevy, so we shone pure Technicolor inside that busy, faded place. We seated ourselves in a middle booth.

"Must be hot out there," our waitress said. She had the kind of stiff blond hair that stayed styled no matter what. "Judging by you ladies' high color."

"Thank you kindly." Momma looked up from the menu,

smiled around at the onlookers as if we were queens on a float. "We'll have toasted club sandwiches with chips and pickles, and two Coca-Colas."

I felt her looking at me, meaning it was time.

I'd been focusing on the table's Formica pattern, waiting for it to blur, getting inside myself. Once I made it there, here came the future, pages of it, fluttering A to Z and back again, coming to a halt at F.

I croaked a monotone message to our waitress. "Your name is Fawna. You were named by a family member. You have one child or more."

Silence inflated the diner like a silver balloon.

"You are sick to death of flat tires." I thought I was finished, but the smell of apricot blossoms boomed inside my senses. I fumbled with words that made no sense to me. "You . . . you . . . will save the day for a crazy–no, *cozy*–girl next spring."

My eyes popped open and Momma squeezed my hand.

The waitress had strong features and I was betting a strong mind to go with them. She looked down at the name tag pinned crooked to her uniform: FAWNA. She frowned, doubting I was on the level. Then she considered the other things. It was true she'd been named by her very own father; and what about that she had one or more kids!

The customers were looking at each other, nodding. One man at the counter even tipped his hat at me.

An elderly lady with stocky lace-up shoes said, "The flat tire part's the topper, Fawna–this morning's must of been the fifth blowout this month!"

Fawna grinned and nodded. "Praise God, she's the real McCoy!"

There was some clapping.

"Be darned . . ." The owner-cook shook his bald head in amazement. "No charge on the toasted clubs for the lovely lady and her large girl."

Naturally, we decided to settle there.

We sat a long time in our booth, reading over and over the "Cot Classifieds," like something new would appear.

Fawna finally caught on to our plight.

"You folks planning on settlin' here? 'Cause if you're looking for a place to rent, you won't find it in the *Cot Herald*. Here in Cot, it's word of mouth and who you know."

She winked and plucked a key out of the cash register. "Only one place in town available."

She pointed the way, said she'd call the building's owner, have him meet us there.

We couldn't say thank you enough.

We got directions to the main street through town— Flowers Street—flowers, just like on our car! There it was, a wooden two-story building! Maybe a little worn down, but it fit in just right with the rest of the block. Upstairs a sign said, Arthur's School of Dance. Piano notes pumped out an open window, along with loud, cheerful-strict words of instruction. I peeked through its separate glass door. Arrows lined the narrow stairway, even though there was no other way but up. Our key clicked open the bottom storefront door, no problem. It had been a butcher shop:

one single long room, the rear end of it turned into an apartment.

Seemed like it hadn't been rented for a long time. Meat-type things were still scattered around: rusted butcher knives, a sign that said DRUMSTICKS 5¢ EVERY TUESDAY, and a giant steel meat grinder me and Momma couldn't budge. Momma threw a heap of stained white aprons straight into the trash, even though it wasn't for her to do.

The back windows were hidden behind heavy navy-blue velveteen curtains that made the kitchen feel underwater. The floor was the outstanding feature. The linoleum was hardly chipped and was patterned with large heads and shoulders of Hopalong Cassidy, my favorite cowboy star.

I guess that got to Momma too. When the owner tapped politely on the open door, she said real positive, "We'll take it."

She asked our new landlord, Mr. Mylo, would he be paying water and electric, then opened her pocketbook and dished out everything but a few one-dollar bills. I tugged at her sleeve in alarm.

"We got to land somewhere, Baby Girl," she whispered to me. "You just watch, this is going to work swell for us."

Mr. Mylo had driven up in a brand-new four-door Lincoln Continental and looked to be the main tycoon in Cot.

He had gray hair brushed back from his big somber head, but his body was on the small side, tidy and just right for wearing quality business suits. Even I could tell his ties were all the right colors—dull ones that made a good impression.

Out of the blue, a vision came to me. I blurted out, "Your niece will soon marry a man with promise."

He shook his head, his brown eyes remaining unsurprised. "That's a fine notion, young miss. But it's been three years since our Sarah Jane's been favored with a beau."

If I didn't have sharp sight, I probably wouldn't have seen the little red sparkle go off in his eyes. Meaning, I'm guessing, he was a little bit tickled, or else he thought he'd just met a kook.

Soon as he drove off, Momma smiled around like she was already seeing the place fixed up.

"There." She pointed to a spot near the front window. "Right there we'll set up the Singer." She put her arm around me and sighed. "We never would have found this opportunity without you making us popular at the diner. You can retire now, honey, let me take care of things."

I surprised myself by saying, "I believe I'd like to keep on giving my Gift to others, Momma. Help you bring in the bacon."

"Okay, honey, if that's what you want. You'd be my first choice anyway, as a partner in business."

Momma was the best when it came to making me feel important.

First thing, she took down the velveteen curtains. The kitchen brightened right up and we now had a view of the red-brick alley. She washed the curtains in the tub, smoothed them as they dried and used them to divide our new space into three areas.

Up front would be her sewing shop.

The small dark middle part was where I would reveal my Sight. I set it up real nice with two chairs and a covered crate with storm candles on top. I thumbed through a left-behind magazine, hoping to find a picture of Elvis for decoration. Only it was a church magazine and there was nothing but Jesus. I chose a picture of him where no blood showed and pinned it to my velveteen wall for luck.

Even though we called the back room the kitchen, it had all the basics of a house: stove, Frigidaire, a chrome-legged eating table, dishes and pots and pans, a bathtub, and a bed that was built into the wall and had to be pulled down. Momma called it the Murphy, like it was a relative of ours. We slept together on the Murphy, which was a treat.

Out in the alley were trash cans and all the cats you could want. A stiff-haired white one with no hearing always let me pick him up.

Momma, who had a talent for stretching money, used one of our dollars to stock us with peanut butter and bread and milk and bananas.

We got ourselves settled in, then painted a business name on the glass storefront, using the gold paint left over from the car:

✶ _BETTINA'S DESIGNS_ ✶
True Forecasts by Baby Girl with Each Fitting

We seated ourselves inside the shop, admiring the backward lettering on the window and waiting for customers to start coming through the door.

33

Our upstairs neighbor was a gangly and red-haired young man who taught tap dance, ballet and acrobatics in his studio apartment. Two nights a week he gave Adult Ballroom lessons. Those were our favorite nights, when waltzes dripped down through the ceiling like water. Listening to the overhead scuffle of earnest feet, Momma and me couldn't help but pull down the shades and dance along. We spun around her dress forms like we were birds. Sometimes I'd pick her up by the waist and twirl her, make her whoop out loud. I loved being so strong.

I knew I'd be a hit in my new school, maybe even more than I'd been in junior high. Here, ninth grade was put in with high school, something that shocked me and Momma at first. I felt too young for that, and had a time picturing myself there.

I was changing, though. Like one funny thing that had started to happen. When I thought back to eighth grade, it wasn't so much my girlfriends I thought about anymore. It was the boys. Guys I'd never even spoken to grew strangely vivid in my mind. And of course my love for Elvis was stronger than ever before. Maybe because I worried for him being inducted into the Army. My stomach would knot with longing, just hearing "Love Me Tender" coming out the diner jukebox. The way he had of making me know I was the one, even though we still hadn't met in person.

My daydreams were different too. Now Elvis not only sang to me, he kissed me and we rolled around some. I spent quite a bit of time between when I went to bed and when Momma came to bed imagining that. I'd dream he'd be waiting for me, parked in his convertible Cadillac outside my old school. We'd both be somehow the right age for dating each other.

"Elvis Aaron Presley!" I'd run down the steps, petticoats flouncing, Official Elvis Pocketbook clutched in my hand. "Don't tell me you took a break from the army just to be with me!"

"Couldn't keep away, li'l mama. Say, aren't you lookin' good! I . . . I . . . been so lonely, I could die."

"Oh, Elvis! When do you have to go back in uniform?"

"I'm staying here, baby." He'd give me his killer smile. "I just wanna be your teddy bear."

In my daydream, it'd be okay to have a date on a school night. It would suddenly be after dark, and we'd be at the drive-in watching something sexy, like Doris Day in pj tops.

Stars would shine overhead and the blue moon would turn to gold.

Elvis would put his arm around me and say, "Treat me like a fool, treat me mean and cruel, but love me."

There would *no doubt* be a kiss.

He'd murmur, "I want you, I need you—"

"—I love you," I'd finish, and then I'd let him move his genuine Elvis Presley hand down to the spot on my chest where I'd miraculously grown a boob.

Next thing you know, we're tying the knot, and ten million heartbroke girls are jumping off the bridge.

These thoughts made me almost sick with feeling, but I went ahead and kept having them.

Meanwhile, actual things were beginning to happen.

One day, the bell tinkled and there was Artie, the dance instructor, coming downstairs to be our first guest. Momma was working near the front window, enlarging my denims through the seat. I was on the floor with the white cat on my chest. He lived with us now, though Momma drew the line at letting him sleep on the Murphy. I was trying to get his claws unhooked from my rayon blouse before she saw him making holes.

Our visitor smiled, giving us a view of the gap between his front teeth. He said, "Look here, the prettiest two flowers on Flowers Street." The tooth gap gave certain words a whistle. "Artie Lemon at your service."

Momma percolated coffee and the two of them sat at the kitchen table and chatted like old friends while I made toast for refreshments.

Artie sat with his rubbery dance-legs wrapped around the chrome legs of his chair, his arms cocked behind the vinyl back cushion. That and the whistle made him seem the happy-go-lucky type.

He said the ballroom dancing was going steady, but it was not the hit he'd hoped it would be when he started up a year ago. He'd envisioned Friday Night Free Forms, and semiannual balls open to the paying public.

I told you about Momma getting bold. She came straight up with a brainstorm.

There were already two seamstresses in town who sewed ordinary school clothes, turned collars, put in new zippers.

All of a sudden, Momma hit on being different. She'd specialize in dance dresses! Help promote the idea of lessons and glamorous cotillions.

This idea suited both Momma and Artie from the get-go.

I could see from the line down Momma's forehead she was thinking on something. I followed at her heels as she rummaged around for the almost-empty can of gold paint, then strode through the door to the sidewalk and added to our sign.

Ball Gown

✳ *BETTINA'S DESIGNS* ✳

True Forecasts by Baby Girl with Each Fitting
Recital Costumes / Formals / Tuxedo Rentals

She hesitated only a second, then stepped up to our sign and added MISS in front of BETTINA'S, even though it made that line off-kilter.

She gave me a strong look and said, "You can be Miss no matter if you're separated or divorced . . . or a widow woman. Anyone without a husband can be Miss."

"That's what I heard too, Momma."

Momma's idea worked like a dream. Artie advertised his first dance in the local paper and made sure it said "proper ball clothes required." This gave Momma plenty of business. Everyone seemed to prefer her reasonable prices to having to sew costumes themselves. While Momma sewed, I painted dance shoes Candy Apple Red.

When she was busy fitting kids for their special outfits, I led their mothers into my velveteen room and gave them readings.

There was only one calamity, and it came right off the bat. I guess my Sight was feeble on that particular day because I misread a woman's future. She was a very attractive woman with goldy-brown pin curls who'd brought her boy for a costume fitting. Inside my head, her page was wide open, the future waiting to be read. She was married to a chipper old man. Then I *thought* I saw her in the high school boys' locker room, beset by a large red-faced man. He was bulky in a sweat suit and had her down on the floor. He urgently walloped her with his hips as she beat her legs in the air, crying *Oh my! Oh my! Oh!*

I was describing the details humping behind my closed lids when she brought me around with a pinch.

Her lips were pressed tight. "You've got someone else's future going there, you overgrown fibber. Why would Coach Bilbo be doing those things? To someone like me?" She whispered real harsh, "Don't you ever repeat that trash, young lady, do you hear me?"

"Come on, Dempster!" She stomped off with her boy in tow.

I told Momma everything. She smoothed my ringlets and said, "Oh, my poor Baby Girl. What have we got you into?"

"You're not peeved I scared off a client, Momma?"

"We're not so hard up we need excitable clients, honey."

I stayed with the readings, and Dempster's mom was the only one who left in a huff.

Momma's confidence stayed full-blown. It turned out she had a head for business. Since she was a Ball Gown Specialist, people didn't come in off the street expecting her to have aisles of fabric, stacks of patterns, buttons and rickrack to choose from. She required Advance Notice and Money Down for her Custom Designs.

She'd cut pictures from fashion magazines, glue them into a scrapbook labeled "Dance Dresses." All her clients had to do was turn the pages and choose a style. Miss Bettina herself would cut the pattern, see to the flattering details that would be unique, guaranteed, to their garment. In this way, she did not have to invest in an inventory of fancy cloth that would just sit around gathering dust.

One day a week we drove the Chevy to Centerville and bought supplies to fill new orders. Momma explained how once she got her reputation, she'd be able to do this by telephone and get everything delivered right to our door.

A catalog arrived from a rental company so we could give clients a choice of tuxedos and accessories. The first one ordered was by Mr. Mylo. For attending his niece's wedding!

He nodded his heavy head. "One more month of college and Sarah Jane's fiancé will be a Certified Public Accountant." He almost smiled, first time I'd seen that. "Just like you foretold, young miss—a man with promise."

Cot wasn't a rich town, but it did all right. It was on the road to ElfLand, a place Momma and me planned to visit someday, to get ourselves some amusement. Because of

ElfLand, both Flowers Street and Mylo Boulevard got good traffic. This and the apricot crop kept money coming in. Cot's citizens wouldn't have minded spending some of it entertaining theirselves. There'd been complaining on how things weren't like they used to be in that department.

The town once had a past full of recreation and highlights. We heard from clients how the waitress Fawna's dad used to fiddle twice a month at St. Edith's Church, St. Edith being the Female Saint of Apricots. He drew himself quite the crowd before he lost his hand to the blades of an apricot pitter. Also there'd been the Bowling Palace, popular till it burned to the ground, and an Armenian Festival that served a goulash supper. Everything had petered out except the drive-in movie, and that was only in the summer.

All that was left to do was eat at the diner or go to one of the run-down bars along Hootchers Alley, where no one would be caught dead.

The time was right for Balls, and you could say Momma started it all. Well, Momma and Artie. By the time school started, Friday nights in Cot meant dress-up dancing for young and old, complete with Hawaiian Punch and Nilla wafers.

Momma and I always went in our latest outfits. Sometimes we danced together, sometimes she danced with Artie, who everyone said was better than Fred Astaire.

Leave it to Momma to already know a complete variety of steps. Other men asked her to dance, but she declined to do it with any men known to be husbands.

I danced with Momma or Artie. In between, elderly

ladies whisked me into a corner, sloshed cups of punch at me and sat too close when they talked. Elderlies were drawn to me like flies, and I came to dread them. I first supposed it was my blond hair and the beautiful blue of my eyes that brought them. The baby-broadness of my face.

It wasn't. Sooner or later, it was always the future they wanted from me.

"Just a peek, dear." They'd rub their bent fingers as if they wanted to snatch it out of me. "Just one little clue."

I stayed firm, answering just like Momma had instructed me: "I do apologize, ladies, but the Future only comes with a Fitting."

CHAPTER 5

———◉———

Breakthrough?

Summer was going. I had the tickle I got the end of every August, craving the surprises of a new school year. I'd seen a few girls around town. Each time, I wondered, would this be a special new friend? Devoted to me like my old girl-friends?

One of them wore a chiffon scarf around her neck with "Elvis Forever" printed on it. That set my heart to thumping! Would she be the one to take Penny's place?

She looked hard at my heavy felt circle skirt, appliquéd with guitars and heartbreak hotels and blue suede shoes. Finally she gave me a small "Hey," the word for hello in Cot, and walked around me. I feared she felt outdone.

Then came a breakthrough.

I was at the diner having a double order of fries and admiring Fawna over behind the counter. She had a whole new head of hair today. Bright red, with curls down her back, three times longer than when I saw her last. A wig! I thought she was clever, giving herself a variety of looks. I wished I had a few wigs myself.

An older teenage girl interrupted my thoughts. She said, "Pleased to have you and your mom move here," and sat down across from me. "I saw you running down the block the other day. Your legs looked sturdy . . . *swift*." She smiled a shy dimpled smile.

Her face was round and pale and solid as the moon and her dark hair framed it off with a pixie cut. Something about that smile of hers made her darling.

Everyone who passed our booth said, "Hey, Cozy!" or "Long time no see, Cozy!" Like the whole town was in love with her.

Even Fawna's pretty calico cat, who lived at the diner but was bashful, jumped up next to her and purred.

Cozy rubbed it in all the best places. I couldn't reach the cat myself, but I joined Cozy in talking to it in a high voice.

"Who's the prett-i-est *kitt*-y?" and

"Best wittle *thing!*"

Stuff like that.

She told me she was a junior in high school, without making it seem like bragging, and pointed out certain kids as they passed outside the diner window. We were having a regular powwow.

43

"That's Charlie Fescue, all-around star of team sports."
Then she nodded at two pretty girls. "The Llewellen
cousins. Personality plus."

She finished her Coke and stood up. "You're really going
to like Cot High. The kids are swell."

It wasn't till she moved to the door that I saw
she limped and wore one of those braces that means polio.

"*'Nice'*"–Fawna shook her head fondly–"hits the nail on
the head when it comes to Cozy Strickland."

I nodded earnestly, went back to twirling fries in catsup.

Boys were a different story. Sometimes Momma and I
passed small groups of them downtown. We noticed there
were two types: hair slicked straight back and hair mowed
lawn-flat.

They'd murmur, "Woo-hoo" and "Yowee" when we went
by, making me feel like the belle of the ball.

Of course some of the fuss was probably over Momma.
Sometimes I felt like whistling at her myself. She was always dressed to beat the band, wearing her pearlized pop-
beads and smelling of Jungle Gardenia.

"Shall I walk you to school tomorrow?" Momma was
putting the last stitches into the shiny taffeta back-to-
school outfit I'd designed for myself.

"Sure, Momma. Way we always do." I was sharpening
pencils, my white cat batting at the wood curls peeling
down to the floor.

I'd named him Starch because of his stiff white coat and because starch was my favorite food group.

Not that he could hear a thing, but I croaked along to him as I screwed a wicked-sharp tip on another pencil. "Good boy, Starch, old Starchy-starch, kitty that I love the most, kitty I'll never let get roasted to ashes—"

I suddenly heard myself and looked up at Momma. She was staring at me. We didn't say a thing about what it was we were thinking.

Next day we were up at the crack of dawn. Momma prepared a hearty oatmeal breakfast for me and braided and pinned up my hair just as I instructed. I added an extra petticoat under my dress, then shucked it back off. Reminded myself not to be the cause of envy, first day at school.

We didn't have a mirror yet, but I got a good impression of myself reflected off the kitchen windows. I twirled around and around, skirt flying out, peacock colors flashing in the early morning light. Momma smiled at me, finished packing my Elvis lunchbox, filling its Thermos bottle with ice and perfume-smelling Kool-Aid. Aunt Lubmilla's yellow-eyed angel gleamed from where it sat on the Murphy. I gave it a pat for luck.

I didn't say a word on the way to school, I was so excited.

Two blocks down, one block to the right, and there it was! A handsome two-story brick building that suddenly loomed with importance. Over its door was carved, COT HIGH SCHOOL, WHERE BOYS ARE ATHLETES AND GIRLS ARE APRICOTS.

Kids milled around the front door. A few leaned against the columns or sat on the wide steps; most were making their way inside.

I knew from Cozy that the tallest, cutest blond boy was Charlie Fescue. He stood in the center of a group of other tall, cute boys. He was built like he'd taken a Charles Atlas course. His hair dipped over his forehead in a way that made me want to smooth it back.

His head snapped toward us.

"Ringa-dinga-*dong*!" he said. "What a dish!"

The other boys gawked.

I smiled evenly across their faces, trying not to miss anyone. Last thing I wanted was broken hearts.

"Okay, Momma," I said real low. "I can do the rest by myself."

"Bye, honey." She knew not to reach for my hand, squeeze it in front of the others.

The closer I came, the wider the boys' eyes got. I swished by them and up the steps, the stiff fabric of my skirt loud in the sudden silence.

A small sweet-faced familiar-looking boy bowed from the waist and hauled open the door for me. Before I could say thank you, the racket of eager voices inside the hall caused me to step back. I looked over my shoulder just as Momma turned the corner and disappeared. For just a second I panicked, eyes casting around for something to give me confidence. I settled on the small boy holding the door for me. He'd carefully parted his brown hair, used water to comb it off to one side. He lifted his down-turned eyebrows in encouragement.

I nodded. The heft of my golden crown of braids gave me the forward stride of a princess.

This was the moment I'd been waiting for. . . .

CHAPTER 6

---◆---

Mean As Snakes

Instead of landing in a magical kingdom, it was more like I'd landed on Mars.

The entire student body was gathered there in the school hall, waiting to race off to first class, claim a seat next to friends. Because of course everyone but me *had* friends. They were real noisy about making that clear. There were shouts of *hey* and *howdy,* high-pitched shrieks, and break-outs of football cheers. Most of the greetings stayed girls to girls and boys to boys. I was relieved to see that, since I wasn't up on boy-girl conversations yet.

If anybody was in charge, it didn't show. There was just the one teacher, reading off last-minute homeroom assign-ments from behind a half-door that led to the school office.

Girls wriggled in tight groups, ponytails of every color and length bouncing in wild competition. Skinny, sly-eyed boys gawked at their tight-skirted heinies while pretending to beat each other up.

The small boy who'd opened the door for me had moved off to a corner. It came to me it was Dempster! Whose mom left the shop in a snit because of my Sight of her with Coach Bilbo. I couldn't believe Dempster was in high school, but I couldn't believe I was either!

He quietly juggled three tennis balls. He was real good at it. I was pretty sure it was forbidden to toss balls inside the building, but that's what he was doing.

I spied Cozy Strickland sitting on one of the steps, and about fainted with relief! She was surrounded by other older girls, but I somehow knew if I could make it to her, she'd let me in the circle. She saw me and reached her hand high to wave at me. On her wrist, a charm bracelet jiggled in the brown light of the hall.

A charm bracelet! It struck me as the classiest touch in the world.

I tried shouldering over to her, but it was so tight and wild in there I might as well have been in a Waring blender.

My brain started to rattle.

Dempster suddenly went into a fancier routine, ricocheting balls off the wall, onto the floor and back into his small hands, but you couldn't even hear the smack over the din of voices.

Then Charlie Fescue pushed through the door, followed by his gang.

A hush fell. Girls shifted in their clothes for his attention, blushed when they got it.

Kids moved aside as he walked across the hall.

I couldn't believe it, but he was coming directly to me! It was like we were in a movie! He smiled and made kind of a question with his eyebrows. I wished I'd asked Momma ahead of time, was I allowed to accept dates this year?

I smiled back.

"Hey," he said. I inhaled the thick V05 smell coming off his yellow hair.

Everyone turned to watch.

"Hey," he said again. "You really Miss Bettina's kid? Or you adopted or something?"

"What do you mean?" I noticed his eyes were the frozen blue of a skating pond.

"We were just wondering—your ma being such a knockout—what happened to you?"

I felt like one of those goldfish dropped in a glass of Coca-Cola.

I croaked, "My mother and I are both Lettish—we're practically *identical twins*."

I knew the second I said it, those were the stupidest possible words in the whole world.

"Lettish and tomato!" someone honked.

"Oh, yeah." Charlie was nodding real seriously. "I can see that now. Identical twins . . . and from the squeezebox sound of you, you probably got a real nice singin' voice too."

It was like I floated out of my body, looked down on

myself with new eyes. Noticed all the girls but me wore sweater sets with belted straight skirts and heavy white bucks on their small feet. I was iridescent as a full-skirted June bug and wore wide patent leather Mary Janes.

Why did I have Momma braid my hair so tight, so perfect, this morning, and pin it on top of my head like I planned to be Queen of Cot High School?

I saw my mistakes adding up! I wasn't ready for high school—

Charlie tapped me on the shoulder, and I plopped back into my body.

Looking into his frozen mirror eyes, I saw myself distorted into a penguin.

His gang stood behind him, faces tight with held-in laughter.

"So—if you're the *twin* of your mother, guess you'll be going to Hollywood, taking the place of Marilyn Monroe—"

"Leave me alone," I tried to say. But if you've ever heard a whole school laughing like a pack of hyenas, you can imagine how my words were drowned out.

Only one voice sounded like a human being.

"Hey, *kids*!" It was Cozy. "She's new—you don't want to give her the wrong impression—"

The laughter worsened, drowning out the excellent point she was making.

I broke away and ran for the girls' lavatory. The heavy door opened onto a billow of cigarette haze. Inside, the room swirled with dimness, like I was about to enter

51

Hades. Only one girl was in there. A tall brownish girl who slouched against the tile wall, sucking on a Lucky like she was starved for smoke. She didn't even look up when I ran in. It was like nothing could scare her into flinching, not even getting caught breaking a serious school law.

I scuttled into a stall, hurled my book bag on the floor and locked myself in. I about choked from the stink of tobacco.

The first bell rang.

The smoker called in to me, voice sharp as broken glass. "New girl? Don't you know kids're meaner'n snakes?" Even through the stall, I could hear her puffing. "Guys *are* snakes. . . ." She mumbled something else I didn't catch.

I didn't answer anyway. I didn't plan to speak again the rest of my life.

"New girl? You stayin' in there forever? You get to class late, they really going to poke fun at you."

The door *shushed* and I knew she was gone. I waited about ten seconds, then held my breath and barreled out through the blue layers of smoke.

The halls were empty. My first class was clear upstairs, but my excellent, hearty legs got me into a seat before the tardy bell quit.

The teacher called roll.

"Bad Girl?" She frowned at the list.

"Present," I croaked. "Only it's Baby Girl."

She scratched at her list, shaking her head like "Baby Girl" made no more sense than "Bad Girl."

"It's a special name," I said, wishing I didn't have to explain. Wishing I didn't have to *exist*.

One of Charlie Fescue's chums sat behind me, wearing a tall red crew cut and a tricky smile. I remembered him because of the chicken way he moved his neck, and the shiny chicken-black of his eyes. He sniggered, tossed a crumpled piece of paper in the air, snatched it back.

"Mr. Kaminski," the teacher said, "would you care to come in after school and further entertain me with your clever antics."

It wasn't a question. The room went quiet.

The teacher shifted her eyes to me. Took in my solid shape, my tight old-fashioned hairstyle and shiny homemade dress. She saw with patient, teacherly eyes that I was not someone who wanted to be more of a spectacle than I already was.

"Fine." She nodded. "Welcome to Cot High, Miss Girl."

"Miss *Girl* . . . !" The Kaminski boy breathed laughter, but only I could hear it.

The teacher went back to calling off names.

The best part of that day was when the history teacher said we'd be studying a great scientist and musician from Latvia named Dr. Rååbit.

"Does anyone know what a citizen of Latvia is called? No? Ah! Someone thinks they do—umm, Betty Girl?"

"*Baby* Girl—"

"Oh my, someone has quite a sore throat—"

"No," I croaked. "Someone is fine. The answer is Lettish."

"Excellent, Betty! Citizens of Latvia—and their language—are called Lettish. Dr. Rååbit wasn't the only notable from there. Some of the great minds in history have been Lettish."

That was news to me! I wondered if Aunt Lubmilla had been a great mind. I caught the redhead's beady black eye and gave him a triumphant look.

He just smirked and said real low, "Rååbits don't speak Lettish, they eat it! Haw, haw."

So my best moment wasn't a real long one.

I told Momma everything went swell at school. She cocked her head for details, but I said I was tuckered and wanted to go to bed.

"Baby Girl? Sweetheart?" She was piled under a wave of sequined fabric, speaking around a mouthful of pins. "It's only four in the afternoon . . . you haven't even had supper—you never miss supper—"

"It's okay, Momma. I don't 'spect I'll be eating anymore."

In the back room, using a hand mirror, I studied myself circle by circle. I saw I was more a curiosity than anything.

I ended up with the face. My eyes were still Momma's brilliant blue, but their shape was narrower than hers. I knew this was due to my lifetime habit of squinting, trying to keep the world in sharp focus. But it was round eyes I wanted, like hers. And my brows were heavier than Momma's. In fact, mine had become two yellow versions of my dad's mustache.

How had I missed that I was looking less like Momma

and more like a walrus? I was no taller than she was. Which came as a surprise since both of us assumed from my bone structure I'd be tall. Instead, here I was, short and thick.

I put the mirror down, laid back on the Murphy and closed my eyes. I tried looking into my own future to see how my suddenly miserable life would turn out.

Not even a preview came to light my way.

The next morning, first I'd heard of it, a pair of girls showed up to walk me to school. Two of Momma's clients, the sisters Helen Llewellen and Loolie Llewellen, who were married to a set of brothers, sent over their two daughters. Momma had set it up. I frowned at the idea of kids being made to get me. Still, we were on Flowers Street, the main road to school, so it wasn't like they were going out of their way.

They turned out to be the famous Llewellen Cousins that Cozy had once pointed out to me. They looked a lot alike: same ginger hair, willowy waistlines, and long legs.

"Nice puff sleeves," Ellen said to me.

There'd been no time between yesterday and today for me to make up a new wardrobe.

"Yeah," said Mary Lou, "you could win a prize on Lawrence Welk or something, dressed like that."

They flashed eyes at each other, as if I didn't know what that meant. As if I were blind.

"We're junior cheerleaders," Mary Lou said. "Which near one hundred percent of the time leads to being a full-blown cheerleader."

I nodded, seeing the importance of this.

She smiled like a lightbulb: on, off.

"Those are nice teeth," I said.

Both the girls turned their heads and opened their lips to give me a better view of their pearlies.

"We had braces!" they said together.

Ellen said, "Me and Mary Lou had to go to Centerville the first Tuesday of every month for three years—"

"Two years, eight months," Mary Lou interrupted.

Ellen frowned. "Whatever—"

"You always exaggerate—"

"I do not—anyway, now we're perfect."

They nodded their heads, back in accord.

Soon as school came into sight, they said, "Here we are, guess it's time to split up? Since we have different things to do than you do?"

I nodded, understanding they didn't want to be seen with me.

I slowed my pace, they quickened theirs, rushing ahead to the shrill greetings of other popular girls.

I stood on the front steps, not wanting to go through the doors. Quite a few kids were doing the same, lingering until the last minute. But only one other was alone. The small boy Dempster.

He was on the opposite end of the entryway, a good distance from me. I couldn't see exactly what he was up to, but he looked to be doing tricks with some kind of a tiny animal. It popped out of his pocket, disappeared, then came running out his sleeve. A pet sneaked into school! Dempster didn't seem to give a hang about rules. I guessed his looks kept the teachers from thinking he was a troublemaker.

It was more than his delicate body. He had big golden-brown baby-eyes, baby-fine hair and a rounded-oval face. Next to deaf cats, I'm partial to babies and anything that looks like one.

His furry creature leaped from one outstretched hand to the other. I wondered what Dempster's secret was, being so satisfied with nothing more than himself for entertainment.

The bell startled me out of staring, and all of us trooped inside. I was relieved to see the hall was orderly today, the kids practically tiptoeing around their lockers. Relieved until I saw why: the principal loomed within the frame of his office doorway. The hunch of his huge shoulders and his tiny unlashed eyes gave him the look of a shark. He turned his head side to side. The bulging forehead made me think something besides a brain was in there.

He greeted the athletes with a few fond rumbly words, whispered in the ear of giggly cheerleaders. But when a gangly, stick-thin boy made the mistake of mock-saluting him, the principal grabbed him violently by the jacket, hauled him inside the office and slammed the door. We heard the small sound of tears and fled the hall.

My relief turned to worry, though nothing much else happened the rest of the day. No one made fun of me. No one even knew I was alive.

Something about lonesomeness made me hungry. That next month I acquired the milk shake habit, heading to the diner each afternoon soon as school let out. If I got there quick enough, I had Fawna all to myself. She'd make me a shake and I'd be out of there before the other kids strolled in from cheerleading and football practice.

Until the day Coach Bilbo canceled practice and I got caught. Charlie Fescue and his teammates banged open the door and plunked down at the counter. I was hunkered in the corner of my booth, so they took the diner to be empty. They drank cherry Cokes, sassed Fawna and bragged about French-kissing some girl with a reputation.

Then I accidentally slurped the last of my shake. At the sound, the whole row of them swiveled on their stools.

"Cheez Louise," Charlie said. "It's Marilyn Monroe, right here in Cot! Stand up and let us see your figure, Marilyn—"

"Yeah!" said the redhead, his neck pushing in and out like a rooster. "Stand up, Marilyn—let us see your two big—"

Fawna leaped from behind the counter, flapping her white apron like a fierce mother goose.

"Pay up and get out! You're nothing but creeps, ever' one of you. Go on now, git!"

They jostled outside. "Bye-bye, Baby *Squirrel*—!"

The bell on the door clanged, like even the diner was laughing at me.

Fawna unscrewed her face, but her makeup stayed wrinkled. "Don't think a thing about those boys, honey. They're nothing ... and besides, you got your mom's blond hair, that's enough beauty for anyone."

58

I stormed out without leaving a tip, pushing past her like she was the one who'd broke my heart.

Charlie Fescue and his gang had a lot to do with the last of my confidence shrinking away. It went down a notch every time I was forced to pass one of them in the halls or on the street. Before long, my self-regard was the size of a peppermint Life Saver. It didn't help that I'd started biting my nails or that I was munching Oreos nonstop, trying to calm my nerves.

Even Elvis was no comfort. Hearing him sing on the car radio just made me miss Penny. It had gone on too long, waiting for Elvis and me to get together. The way he'd sung his heart out, making it seem like it was just for me? It wasn't. My heart stung, seeing the falseness of his promise. I wondered if Penny had caught on yet. I yearned to know.

I asked Momma, could I write her, at least have us be pen pals? And what about Beverly and Madeline?

She pressed her lips together, considering. "I thought that myself, about writing to our fine old landlady. It wasn't right, us having to take off in the night like that, not able to say goodbye."

We nodded at the memory.

"But then I thought, what if it got back to . . . *him*? Where we were?"

We frowned.

"I 'spect it's not worth the chance, is it, Momma?"

"I 'spect not."

Me and Momma didn't have too many talks about the

past. Even this one set her to silently patting Aunt Lubmilla's pillow, me to petting Starch.

I can't even think why Ellen and Mary Lou kept coming by to pick me up for school. My best guess was that Cozy, who had to be driven to school herself, asked them to do it. I'd seen the three of them, heads together in the hall. Cozy gestured my way, smiled at me in her comforting manner. The Cousins glanced at me with a shamed look, which goes to show the powerful influence Cozy's goodness had on people.

I became a sort of mascot to the Cousins, like a hedgehog or a Martian. I was surely no more included in their conversations than one.

Sometimes they forgot to come by. When they did come, they were *always* late. Tardiness didn't even seem a bad thing to them. Like junior cheerleaders didn't get report cards or something.

Still, they tolerated me, and that led to some of the others doing the same.

It was enough to save me from being purely forlorn.

CHAPTER 7

Love 'n' More

Froggy is what some of the kids whispered behind my back. Based, I supposed, on my voice, or else me not having an hourglass shape. I heard them say it and they knew it. But who cared, I tried to convince myself, if that's what they thought, or if I didn't have real friends? I'd had enough friends in junior high to last a lifetime! I was older now, and other things were more important.

Like being away from my father.

And bringing up my classwork.

I was distracted and found it hard to concentrate. Things didn't come naturally easy the way they used to. Of course I still had favorite subjects. Two of my three best classes were gym and spelling. Spelling was like falling off a log. Like, along with the pages of people's future lives, I had a dictionary inside me where I could look up anything. Spelling words like *fastigiate* or *skewbald* was no problem, but my mind's dictionary didn't come with definitions and I had no idea what the words meant.

It was a goal of mine to learn, because except for the spelling, my English wasn't too good.

The teacher said work on it because English can come in handy.

Gym was a huge class that included girls from other homerooms. Like always, it was easy for me. The only hard part was trying to ignore the naked bodies in the locker room—girls acting like boobs were no more embarrassing than feet. Most of them had starter sets, but some had full-sized pillows. I of course didn't have a thing, unless you counted the two spots on my chest, no more than closed pink eyes, nipples still shut inside them.

Momma had told me I was from a line of slow bloomers. I had no choice but to cling to this notion.

I wasn't the only one in my condition. I was amazed to see that Mary Lou didn't have anything either! I'd gotten a glimpse of her plain ribs when she dashed for the shower, arms crossed tight across herself. She was the opposite of Ellen in that way. Ellen had one of the plumpest chests in school. Boys leered at her when she walked by, snickered, "Oo-ee, Ellen is swellin'."

The same boys, the cruel ones, said of Mary Lou, "Mary Lou is missing two." This about girls who were practically perfect in their looks!

Luckily, no one noticed what I did or didn't have. I was

invisible—except when I did standing broad jumps or rope-climbed. I could get up that rope faster than an orangutan.

Even the popular sophomore beauty Carline Halsey and her popular beautiful girlfriends were impressed. "Neat-*o!*" they cried.

I swelled with my old feeling of specialness.

There was just one girl better at gym than me: Selda, the only known mulatto in Cot. Meaning she was one part Negro and one part Crustacean, same's the rest of us. She was strong and fierce as a Doberman-style attack dog. And about as popular as one.

She was a guaranteed standout with her long neck and bulging yellow eyes and a style of dress that included neckerchieves and plastic animal clips on the tail of every one of her short braids.

Of course I'd noticed her from Day One: she was the girl smoking in the lavatory. Gym was my only class with her, so I hadn't got my fill of looking at her yet.

It didn't help her any, to be as good at sports as a boy. She was the last to get picked for teams. The kids said she had cooties. If they brushed against her, they'd wipe the invisible germ-bugs off, stick them on someone else. It was kind of a fun game for them. I guess.

If it bothered Selda, you'd never know it. She was cool as a cucumber and not someone you'd feel sorry for.

I secretly admired her for that. Everything about her said, *Don't take one step closer. I don't care if you admire me or not.*

It was that chip on her shoulder that made her—instead of me—the most unpopular girl at Cot High.

On mornings when the Cousins bothered to show up, it'd be about three minutes before the first bell was due to ring. They didn't actually stop, just slowed down while I rushed out to greet them.

"Hey, Ellen! Hey, Mary Lou!"

"Hey." They had a way of taking up the whole sidewalk. I had no choice but to walk behind them, their long-legged pace forcing me to scurry to keep up.

At first I'd call out things I thought would be of interest to junior cheerleaders. "Think we'll win the big game over at Tuber Valley?"

Getting no answer back made me feel a fool. After a while I quit trying and just strained to hear what they said to each other. Stuff that was so darn interesting, nothing I said mattered.

Mostly it was boys they talked about. They used a sort of code. Like "You-Know-Who" or "Hunka Munka."

One day when they saw Dempster cross the street in front of us, they giggled, "Howdy Doody."

I felt for him. Being small for his age was his only crime. Plus he was a tiny bit odd-featured. What was so wrong with being small and odd-featured?

Or being a little short and stout?

Unless you were a teapot, it seemed like everything.

Then one day when Mary Lou was in a specially sticky mood, pretending she was ugly and wanting constant compliments from Ellen, I felt myself slip inside myself. Without even looking for Ellen's page, there it was. A pink page, of course. Halfway down it, a lacy valentine said, *Ellen + Rooster = Love 'n' More.*

I mumbled, "Who's Rooster?"

That got their attention.

Ellen almost shouted, "*Rooster?* Rooster *Kaminski?*"

My vision melted and I was back on the sidewalk.

She was real excited, an unnatural state for her. "He sits right behind you in homeroom, stand-up red hair, randy-looking—"

Mary Lou said, "That's gross, Ellen—watch your mouth!"

I droned, "Ellen Llewellen plus Rooster Kaminski equals Love 'n' More."

"It *does?*" Ellen was all ears. "Who said that?"

"I have the Sight—"

"Oh yeah," Mary Lou said. "Remember, El? That sign on Miss Bettina's shop? That Baby Girl sees the future? Fawna told my mom she was the real McCoy. Creepy—"

Ellen whirled on Mary Lou, eyes overbright. "It's not creepy." She grasped my arm. "Is that strictly true? About me and Rooster?"

Mary Lou planted herself in front of me. "You sure you didn't snoop on Ellen, read her diary or something? She's crazy about Rooster, but he's going with Carline Halsey—"

"That's not for sure, Mary Lou!" Ellen's eyebrows beetled with warning.

"She wears his *sweater,* for Pete's sake."

"I didn't snoop." I wondered if we were talking about

the same Rooster. Why would Ellen go for someone whose red head pecked the air like it was punching holes in it? "I saw it just now. It's the future."

"Oh! Right. The *future*. Like *later* he'd be my husband? Well, I can wait for the future! Can't I, Mary Lou?"

"I guess." Mary Lou moved off from Ellen. "If you don't mind Carline going steady with your make-believe husband."

Ellen said, "Sometimes I hate you, Mary Lou, you know that?"

Mary Lou stomped off and Ellen walked real close to me the rest of the way to school.

I didn't even mind coming in tardy.

At lunch while Ellen was cruising Rooster Kaminski's table, Mary Lou slammed her tray down next to me.

"Okay, Madame Fortune-Teller, if you know so much, what's *my* future?"

I didn't even bother looking inside myself. "Your personality will turn winning and you will be more popular than ever."

She gave a little cat-smile and nodded, like that's just how she saw the future herself. Then she frowned. "Wait . . . I already have a winning personality."

Ellen sat down on the other side of me. "No you don't, Mary Lou. As your cousin, let me be the first to tell you—"

Mary Lou shoved to her feet and moved over to the next table, squeezing herself into the crowd around Dempster. Kids had pushed close to watch him carve something clever out of a stick. It appeared to be an instrument of some kind—a narrow flute or piccolo. His small knife flew down its sides, shaping something remarkable right before our eyes. Dempster's hands seemed bigger than before, oversized on his narrow wrists. I couldn't help but root for him, hoping he'd be like his stick, shape up into something fancy, right in front of the girl who'd called him Howdy Doody.

I shook my head. For a mild little kid, he took a lot of chances. Surely pocketknives weren't allowed? Luckily, the teacher on lunch duty had her hands full trying to get everyone to eat their mushy green beans before bolting for the playground.

Ellen was going on. "*When* in the future, Baby Girl? When will it happen?"

I was real sick of talking about Ellen plus Rooster. I shrugged. I saw she was torn between saying something hateful and being afraid to lose her source of boyfriend information.

She picked at her lunch for a while. "Want my green beans?"

"No."

"Suit yourself."

She went to the gym to practice cheers and I went outside.

There, Dempster was doing some kind of amazing stunt against the side of the school. He'd barrel full-tilt toward it, run up the brick wall about five feet and flip back over to his feet.

Being an athlete myself, I knew that under his oversized clothes he must be accumulating muscles. I stared, trying to memorize the trick for my own use.

I guess he had eyes in the back of his head. Next time he flipped, he sprang around to face me and bowed. I was so surprised, I found myself bowing back.

Ellen showed up by herself the next morning. We walked side by side to school, but we didn't have much to say to each other.

Then the morning after, both Cousins were there. They'd made up again. They hardly paused for me as I rushed out the shopfront.

I tagged along, listening to them whisper and giggle.

Everything was back to normal.

CHAPTER 8

---◆---

A New Voice

Geography was the third thing I excelled in. Since we'd left, I'd kept a close eye on geography, checking again and again where it was we'd left Dad, and where it was we were now. A good long distance every time.

In the map of my mind, the distance was a rigid red line. Passing time had turned it into a one-way road, there to here. No temptation on earth–seeing Penny or Madeline or Beverly or the landlady again, or even if Elvis moved there–nothing could get me to go back anymore.

I think Momma saw it the same. She was vague, talking about past times, even with me. She especially was dodgy about had she gotten the divorce.

"Did we get it, Momma? I sure would like to have that divorce."

"Honey, do I look like I have a husband anymore? That's what a divorce means, not having some husband around you don't want. . . ." She'd trail off like the past had took hold of her and was dragging her into another room.

I figured it would take some kind of contact with Dad to get our divorce and doubted she'd want to chance that. I know for sure I didn't. I was tired of being killed.

The folks in Cot assumed Momma was a widow. She looked like one, so small and appealing, the permanently worried forehead. She never said otherwise.

She seemed happy here, though she didn't have real friends either. Most folks had their socials over at St. Edith's Church. Not being farmers, we had no need to pray about things like blight or apricot beetles. Instead, we kept Sundays for ourselves.

Momma had Artie, and a good acquaintance with Mr. Mylo, and chats with clients. That, put together with me, seemed plenty enough for her.

I sensed her watching me from the storefront on school mornings, the Cousins, heads together, always a few steps ahead of me. Noticing that I always came home alone.

After school, she'd stop whatever she was sewing and give me an extra-tight hug, like I was the most winsome thing in the universe. "Bring home any friend you like, honey. I'm never so busy I can't make up cocoa with marshmallows." Even in a hug, she felt the tiny shake of my head. "Or it can be just the two of us!"

It must have been obvious to Momma, she was the only

one taken with me. No matter what, she stayed loyal. Even when I brought home the first semester's grades. It clearly wasn't the report card of a star. My math grade was plain shameful.

Instead of scolding, she came up with a plan to raise my spirits: she'd enroll me in dance class.

"You've got flair, Baby Girl. A highly rare thing for someone your age."

That was how she put it, adding that an extracurricular activity rounds a girl out.

I could see in Artie's mirrored walls that my dance movements were stumpy. Still, certain polka numbers filled me with joy. I'd take off bouncing around the studio all on my own, mind emptied of things like thick waists, or school, or fathers who lurked like deadly tadpoles in the dark watery moments before sleep.

Artie smiled his gappy smile as he watched me hop around. It gave him an inspiration of his own. He secretly suggested to Momma that his brother Stanley, who owned a shoe store over in Centerville and was a crackerjack accordion player, might give me music lessons.

I didn't know a thing about this idea until Christmas. It came as an absolute surprise, finding a red and silver accordion under the tree. It was the prettiest quality instrument I'd ever seen. Half piano and half pleats, the whole she-bang was meant to be strapped on the front of you, just like a baby. It had belonged to Mr. Mylo's grandmother, and he was so tickled with the idea of me playing it, he let

71

it go for a real sweet price. That's what Momma and Artie told me, smiling their heads off.

I compressed its pleated sides and pushed out an alarming string of notes. Even my white cat flinched, and it was a known fact he was deaf.

"It'll come," Artie said. "Wait till Stanley shows you the ropes."

I knew it was true. This would be my new voice—the clear, harmonic, lovable voice I'd wanted without even knowing it.

That night I was so antsy, thinking about learning music, that I couldn't sleep.

Momma said, "Stop fidgeting, Baby Girl. Turn over on your side and curl up. Count sheep."

"There aren't enough sheep to get me there, Momma."

"Count anything there's lots of, stars in heaven, lines down the road . . ."

Instead I pictured the endless flip of pages, each one telling the story of someone's future. I fell asleep looking for mine.

Just after New Year's, Momma drove me to Centerville for my first music lesson. The roads were slick and we had to go in the dark because Stanley Lemon wasn't available except evenings.

He'd told Momma that on the telephone. "Lemon's Shoe Store can't close till five in the P.M. no matter what."

Momma waited, thinking more explanation was coming. None was.

"Oh," she said. "We sure do understand. Could be an emergency, youngster loses a saddle oxford, misses out on some school?"

"Yes, ma'am."

Momma waited again.

He finally said, "Fifteen after, we'll commence."

Stanley turned out to be a solid older version of Artie, handsome and squared off in a Gene Kelly sort of way. I was guessing he didn't have Artie's gap-teeth, since his words didn't whistle. But he didn't smile much so I didn't know for sure. At first, because of his not smiling, I didn't think I'd like Stanley as well as Artie. Later I found out it was just his way. He had some sadness in him that had to do with being a widower.

Stanley could play music the way Artie could dance to it; they were really something in the music department. Artie swore they didn't get it from any known relatives, it was just a one-time miracle.

Stanley was a real professional. He had written a question down on paper and pointed that I should sit down and write an answer back. This excited me.

Why do you dessire to play the accordion?

"'Desire' only has the one 's' in it," I croaked without looking up from my task.

"That's very observant," Stanley said, his face solemn. "I'll make a note of that."

Momma said, "Baby Girl's smart as a tack."

Stanley blinked at her. Nodded.

I wrote down one sentence.

I wish to get back what my dead father stole from me.

All of us stared at my answer for a while. Then Stanley cleared his throat and began instructing me on the position of my fingers on the cream-colored keys.

Without giving too much praise, he got me learning things. This week's assignment was memorizing notes.

I like to burst on the trip back to Cot. My head was filled with music I'd made myself and words like *chromatic* and *semitone*.

I practiced every day after school, even before I did homework. Everyone said I was a natural. When Mr. Mylo came in and listened to my efforts, he cried like a baby.

Momma dabbed her hanky on his tear-spotted suit, and he lifted his heavy face into a grandfather smile for us. Then, walking his quick walk out the door, he ducked into his ritzy Lincoln and was off.

Something about starting up with music changed me over Christmas vacation. I knew I was still an outsider at school, but I was getting chummy with myself again.

Half the time after that, I went ahead to school without waiting for the Cousins. At least that way I wasn't late.

CHAPTER 9

Girls Are Apricots?

Monday mornings always started with the principal holding special assembly in the auditorium, where the main attraction was the principal himself. We never saw him during the week; if his door opened at all, it meant trouble. There was something thrilling about gawking at him from the safety of our distant seats. Like the field trip I took in third grade, watching giant sharks behind glass.

Usually the point of assembly wasn't much, getting bawled out for lack of school spirit or rallying for coming games. This was the first assembly of second semester, and for a change it was a doozy. The principal wrapped his whacking-big hands around the microphone and made the announcement.

"Something special has come our way, students of Cot High! We're having a teen talent show! It will be held this spring, right on this very stage where I'm standing."

Whoops came on cue.

"Now, now!" he boomed. "I saw a few of you young ladies doing wolf-whistles out there. This is Cot High, 'Where Boys Are Athletes and Girls Are Apricots.' Do apricots wolf-whistle? I don't think so. . . ." He paused a moment, then gave us apricots a small-toothed smile. "*Okay!* Here are the teen talent guidelines. . . ."

Gasps came nonstop as he read them out.

Categories were Music, Gymnastics, Poetry and Unique Talents.

Each act could have one to five students in it.

Nothing dirty could go on.

Nothing could be longer than three minutes.

Cash prizes would go to the two runners-up.

The best act would of course win first prize: an overnight all-expense-paid trip to ElfLand!

Plus! The winners would get their pictures featured on Page One of the school yearbook!

I doubt there was a single person not talking out loud or secretly planning their category. Mine would be Music, of course. I vowed right then to come up with a real special number.

Mary Lou and Ellen were sitting in front of me, arguing in fierce whispers. I caught Ellen saying, "Shaking pom-poms isn't gymnastics! And I'm not going flipping in the air, breaking my neck in front of boys."

"O-*kay* then," Mary Lou said, "I'll write a poem."

"Oh, sure, Madame Shakespeare, I'd like to hear that."

"You don't get it, do you? I am *going* to be featured in the yearbook, period!"

At lunchtime, Ellen, real polite and quiet, set her tray next to mine. To prevent getting snubbed for the millionth time, I didn't even look over at her.

She tapped my shoulder. "Um, Baby Girl? How come you don't wait for us anymore? You mad at me and Mary Lou for something?"

"No."

"Just that we come too late?"

I shrugged.

Mary Lou sat herself across the table from us and was carefully taking everything off her tray and setting the table for herself. Fork to one side, napkin just so, like she was having a steak dinner at a restaurant.

She'd paid an extra nickel for a delicious carton of chocolate milk. Making a show out of doing it, she set it on my tray, complete with straw.

"Think nothing of it," she said.

My mouth flopped open.

Something was up.

"Golly Moses," she said cheerfully. "Guess we'll just have to set the clock for earlier; can't be having you late for school. You eatin' that roll, El? You said you'd rather be dead than get thick in the waist."

Ellen turned pink and locked eyes with Mary Lou.

I pretended the words "thick" and "waist" had nothing to do with me.

"*A-actually,*" Ellen stammered, making things worse, "I'm *trying* to fill out my middle. Boys like that."

"What're you saying, Swellin'—I mean Ellen?" It was Charlie Fescue right behind us, listening to every word! "You saying guys like fat girls?" He was carrying on a conversation with Ellen's chest. "Give me a break, cupcake. Guys don't even like girls that *sit* with fat girls."

And then he was gone.

And so were Ellen and Mary Lou, gathering up their plates of untouched mac 'n' cheese and tough Jell-O squares, acting like I suddenly had cooties. Giving some feeble excuse about having to break in new pompoms.

At the last second, Mary Lou turned and flashed her smile on and off at me. "Catcha later."

That fake smile did not make up for one thing.

I watched Charlie amble off in the other direction. Without my even taking a deep breath, I suddenly got the Sight. Clear as day I saw him driving a Greyhound bus, a man so fat his uniform like to split open. I stared at the vision. Yep, it was Charlie Fescue all right; it said so right there on his name tag.

This should have been more comforting than it was, but vengeance happening twenty years in the future did not help my mood one whit.

I chewed furiously on my roll, concocting a daydream of the Cousins tumbling down the bleacher steps, landing on their heads as they cried, "First Down, Fourth Down, Cot High wants a Touchdown!"

By the time I swallowed the last of my Jell-O, savoring its bitter green aftertaste, I felt better. I'd even made up an original song to play on my accordion, though probably not one I'd use for the talent show. It was more a cheer dedicated to Cot High cheerleaders:

"Kick 'em down the stairs, pull their shiny hairs, hang 'em by the neck and send 'em straight to heck."

I tossed the unopened carton of chocolate milk in the garbage, which like to killed me.

CHAPTER 10

Ry-Krisp and Before-School Friends

That evening, I told Momma I was too tired to go to the market with her, and besides I'd only be eating cottage cheese and Ry-Krisp from now on.

Momma said, "Oh, Baby Girl, you're not taking up fads, are you? Ideas you maybe got from Ellen and Mary Lou?"

"No, Momma. It's just that's all I'm going to eat."

She frowned and went on without me.

Soon as she was gone, I stripped off all my clothes. We didn't have a full-length mirror, so I stood on a chair in the kitchen. It was dark in the alley, so I could see my reflection in the long window. I studied myself real good and was startled to find that where my legs joined up was a patch of crinkly yellow fuzz. I should have been expecting it. I'd seen the other girls in gym. Would it turn dark and roughen up like theirs?

I gave a tug. One hundred percent rooted. I stood there dwelling on myself for I don't know how long.

The rest of me was boring, compared. But there was nothing about me soft or roly-poly. Nothing *fat*. I wished without thinking about it that Charlie could see me like this and admit he was wrong to call me such a thing. I was just a little thick through the middle, with sturdy strength concentrated in my arms and legs. A solid person, like Momma said.

One of the windowpanes had a long wave to it that turned my body into something slender and Bettina-like.

I was staring at the other squares to see if I could find an even more flattering reflection, when my focus suddenly went through the window to the alley. There, nose to the glass, a face stared straight in at me and my foolish nakedness. It was the boldest face in the world, and I feared my stupid wish had come true! That Charlie Fescue was here, watching me, eyes pale as sneering ghosts!

I was so shocked that the face seemed to zoom in, out, in, like I was bouncing inside a telescope! I fell off the stool and cracked my head on the floor so hard I started to cry.

Momma came dashing in from the front, dropping armfuls of groceries and crying out, "Stars in heaven, Baby Girl, you're stark naked and bleeding out the head! What in the world's going on?"

"I was going to take a bath, Momma. I tripped on the chair and busted myself. . . ."

As I sobbed out lies, I kept my eyes glued to the window. Nothing left there but the sight of me and Momma.

The next morning I woke up groggy. The bump on my head hurt like blazes when I tried to brush my hair. I was trying to get a ponytail going when the bell rang up front. I heard Momma say, "Well, good morning. You two are up bright and early."

"Yes, ma'am."

The Cousins.

"We set the clock early so's we'd get to school on time."

"Well, I'll be. Getting to school on time. What next, girls? The honor roll?"

"Yes, ma'am," Mary Lou said earnestly, like she was talking to a beauty pageant judge. "If me and El are going to be pediatricians, I guess honor roll's the next stop."

The Cousins were so used to enchanting everyone, they didn't have a clue Momma was on to them. Guess Momma had got her fill of watching them treat me like I was no-'count.

Ellen must have finally noticed what Momma was working on.

"Jeepers! That's a nifty little party dress you're sewing up!"

"Mm-hmm. This nifty little party dress is for Carline Halsey." I imagined Momma snipping a thread with her little stork-billed scissors. She had real style with those scissors. "I don't know if she plans to go to medical school like you girls, but she definitely plans to be Miss Apricot."

"Oh, she will be." Mary Lou's voice was all sighs and weariness. "The Halsey sisters are always Miss Apricots."

"Mmm," Momma said. "Did you girls pick this morning for being on time for some special reason?"

"Momma!" I hollered, voice like a broken crow. "I'm almost ready. Tell them wait. If they want."

"Hey, Baby Girl!" Ellen hollered back. Then to Momma, "Must be swell, getting to live in a store."

"Oh, it *is*! Positively swell."

I'd never heard Momma so feisty! I pushed through the curtain like I was coming from backstage, saw the way the Cousins were gazing at Momma. They hadn't noticed a shred of mockery, all they saw was that she was beautiful. Like that was Momma's best thing!

"Here she is!" Momma said it like a star had fallen from heaven. "Doesn't that pigtail hurt, honey, stretched over your poor bumped head?"

"It's a *ponytail*, Momma; ponytails don't hurt."

"Well—have fun at school, girls."

"We will!" the Cousins said together. They slipped their arms through mine, just like we were real friends.

Last time they dumped me, I vowed never to get swept away by them again. But walking close between them like this, their high spirits and prettiness started to get to me.

"How now, brown cow," Mary Lou said, once we were out on the sidewalk.

On the other side of me, Ellen gave my elbow a chummy squeeze.

"Mary Lou and me were talking . . . we want you to be our before-school best friend."

"But not *at* school." Mary Lou frowned in a concerned

83

way. "So's not to interfere with your schoolwork, you being such a brain and all."

"So!" Ellen said, sensing I was weakening to their charms. "Next thing you know, it'll be the three of us doing things *after* school!"

"Don't you guys practice cheers after?"

"Not every day, and besides, we got the future to think of."

"Yeah." Mary Lou winked at me. "And Baby Girl's an expert at the future!"

I frowned. Something was definitely going on here. "Are we still dwelling on Ellen plus Rooster?"

They shook their heads, ponytails switching left, right, left.

"What we're *dwelling* on, Baby Girl, is the three of us and our act in the talent show." We'd all stopped on the sidewalk. I suspected we'd be late again. "Me and El dressing up in short shiny costumes, taking questions from the audience, and you sitting in a refrigerator box painted up real nice, calling out the answers."

"Oh."

Their sudden niceness was starting to make sense.

"Come on, Mary Lou." Ellen tugged us ahead. "The important thing is to get our friend to school on time! We'll plan out the details tomorrow morning."

I wished like anything I could see my own future, though I was pretty sure it didn't include me in a cardboard box. My talent was music, pure and simple.

Still, I didn't get around to mentioning it just then. I wasn't too eager to spoil the new part-time friendship I'd let myself in for.

That day in gym class, I was picked out to demonstrate the discus throw. I noticed Selda, thin and sharp as a blade, standing off to the side. My first throw turned out to be a school record. The other girls murmured praise, but Selda just stood there staring at me, meaning I didn't know what.

After school, Carline Halsey stopped at my locker. I couldn't help but stare at her heart-shaped face, gray eyes wide apart and marked with a daisy pattern you don't see every day. I could see she was used to being admired. Her hair was a dark silver-blond turned under in a pageboy. And I swear her figure was better than Gina Lollobrigida. There really was a power to beauty.

"How's my Apricot dress coming along?"

"Good."

Just then the principal came out of his office, passed by us with a wink. "Howdy, young ladies."

"Hello," I croaked.

Carline frowned.

He loomed over us, smiled dreamily at Carline's backside, then aimed an eagerly cupped hand. She jumped aside like she'd known it was coming.

"Quit it, Uncle Hal, that's plain embarrassing!"

The principal chuckled and lumbered on down the hall.

"Wow," I said. "You kin to the principal?"

She made a gesture that didn't mean yes or no. "*Anyway,*

maybe I'll come by your shop, check my dress out. Give you a chance to read my future. Afterward, we'll go have a soda pop or something."

"Okay." I kept my smile a normal size until I was out the door. Then I trotted all the way home, grinning my head off. Practiced my accordion with noisy passion. Beautiful friends before school, beautiful friends after! Maybe my life would work out after all.

———◆———

CHAPTER 11

Selda's Spoons

I had a new thing stuck in my head before sleep. It was both a nightmare and a dream, and it featured Charlie Fescue looking at me as I stood naked on the chair. I knew it hadn't been Charlie's face in the window that night—it hadn't looked a thing like him—but some part of me wanted it to be so. In my vision, Charlie walked right in the kitchen door.

"I see you're not fat, cutie pie," he said. Air sweet with his hair grease. "I see that you are a swell-looking, strong-built gal."

He'd be staring at me and I'd be just standing there, not moving a muscle, watching us in the slimming window-pane.

This played over and over in my mind like a favorite

movie. I was just crazy about the notion. It made me squirmy and moody and . . . something . . . and had nothing at all to do with the mean, smart-aleck Charlie Fescue I saw every day at school.

In real life, I wouldn't let Charlie Fescue touch me with a ten-foot pole.

Carline Halsey did come over to the shop a few days later, just like she said. She was wearing her hair in a perfect French twist and had thin black lines painted next to her lashes, setting off her eyes. Her dyed-to-match wool skirt and sweater were a blend of royal blue and forest green. She looked straight off the cover of *Keen Teen* magazine.

I was practicing "Mockingbird Hill" on my accordion when she walked in.

Momma said, "Well, Carline! What brings you here?"

Carline said, "Well, sort of I came to visit Baby Girl."

"Want to try your dress on, just for fun?"

Carline stepped into the private dressing corner and went down to her slip. "Hope you didn't make the bust too tight. I'm big up top."

Momma smiled at the floor, then helped the dress real careful over Carline's hairdo.

It fit perfect. Carline kept twisting and turning, saying, "How do I look? Pretty? Is the color right?"

She did look pretty, and the color she'd picked was apricot, so naturally it was right.

Momma said, "Baby Girl, we ought to get a tall mirror. People want to see themselves better—"

Carline broke in real rude. "Where do I get my future done?"

She shrugged her dress off and left it for Momma to pick up.

The two of us pushed through the curtain wall, set ourselves down in the dreamy midnight shadows of my velveteen room. Carline tapped her fingers and sighed as I tried to go inside myself.

She might as well have been a Hoover, the way she vacuumed the future out of my head. I swear when I glanced up at my picture of Jesus, he shook his head at me. The two of them racked my nerves so bad, I decided to just pretend. Something I was getting into the habit of doing.

"You will be Miss Apricot." A safe enough prediction.

"I know that," she said. "What about me and Rooster?"

Rooster again! I was trying to think what to make up when my Sight snapped me up. Inside it, there's nothing but truth, and I was no longer in charge of what I said.

"You will be Mrs. Rooster Kaminski and you will live one mile from ElfLand and own a five-room motel."

I came out of it confused. What about Ellen? I'd seen her page clear as day and *she'd* been with Rooster!

Carline was smiling her tight little smile and nodding. "I knew that was gossip, about my Rooster and Ellen. But who would have guessed me and Rooster'd live by ElfLand? Sounds like we're going to the top."

She'd gone all misty and walked out of the shop without a goodbye to Momma or a word about going for that soda pop.

I was so starved I was shaky and decided to break my rule, maybe have some peanut butter and jelly on top my Ry-Krisp. Make some extra for Momma. I carried the snack in, set up a TV tray, so all she'd have to do is reach.

"Momma? Sorry Carline treated you so rude."

"Don't worry, honeybunch." She narrowed her eyes just the way I always did, like we feared their brightness would blind somebody. I could tell by her smile a joke was coming. "We tack on a special extra charge for rudeness. The Halseys are going to have to buy us roast chickens and mashed potatoes from here to China."

My favorites!

I smiled back and, later, practiced my music an extra long time.

By the time I squeezed out the final note, I felt like things were going pretty good.

It caused quite a stir, the morning Selda got "transferred" into my homeroom. Ellen whispered it meant her regular homeroom teacher couldn't put up with her. She said this was because even though Selda didn't say much, she had a know-it-all look on her face.

I glanced over at Selda as we said the Pledge of Allegiance. She blinked the round, slow-moving lids of her eyes back at me, which I took to mean *beware*, but later she said it meant *who are you?*

She was older and taller than the rest of us on account of she'd never once done her homework and they'd flunked her two times. If things had gone right, she'd already be a

90

junior! But when my homeroom teacher, who was teaching adverbs for that day's English lesson, called on Selda, she knew the answers every time. She knew answers even I didn't know. Finally the teacher quit bothering trying to trip her up.

Coming into my homeroom meant Selda's whole schedule changed. She was now not only in gym with me, she was in all my classes. Everywhere I looked, there she was, looking at me without me being able to catch her at it. She even had her lunch the same time as me. Afterwards she'd always stand in the corner of the schoolyard, a tall dark stripe dividing the shadow of the giant larch tree.

This was how I found out she was a musician.

I knew right away this meant trouble, on account of me being a musician too. It's a natural fact musicians get drawn together into bands, even if they don't care to have a thing to do with each other, which we didn't.

Her instrument, I knew, was the spoons. She played them so fast they seemed to spark. Their music chattered across the yard like bullets. She was a perfect wonder with those teaspoons.

Outside in the schoolyard, on account of Selda being so spurning, nobody dared go into her corner. But they couldn't help feel the music of those spoons. They looked off into space, shagging their butts and clogging their feet like it had nothing to do with her.

Even Ellen and Mary Lou and Carline burst into a series of cheerleading deep-knee bends, waving invisible pom-poms in time to those spoons.

"Give me a C–C–C!
"Give me an O–O–O!
"Give me a T–T–T!
"Yay!"

Spelling Cot over and over again in the same annoying way.

I stood halfway between the cheers and the spoons, stiff as a board and wishing I was–I don't know–*wanted* somewhere. That I knew what it was I had to do to get wanted.

Selda's music got to me, that's a fact. But worse, it made me feel something for her. Respect, I guess. Above that, it pleased me that she had power over the popular kids as well, even though they never would have admitted it. It was partly because of Selda that I had the nerve to bring my accordion on Hobby Day. My music, not perfected yet, wasn't a smash hit, but I saw it opened Selda's yellow eyes to me.

After that, I knew somehow it'd be okay to stand near her after lunch and try out some tunes.

I moseyed over to the larch and heard myself say, "I have the Sight."

"Yeah, well . . ." She cupped her spoons and rattled them at me like Tommy guns. "I've seen some sights of my own."

I couldn't do anything like that back, I was new at this, so I started in on "The Plunk-Footed Polka."

Selda sighed, slowed down her spoons like it was killing her, and followed the steady rhythm of my squeezes.

We didn't sound too good, but it was the start of some big changes.

The Cousins marched up to me after the bell called us back in the building.

Ellen said, "What were you thinking, talking to Selda? Don't you *know* about her?"

I knew she smoked. That didn't seem so bad.

"We didn't talk."

"Geez Louise, Baby Girl, you did worse than that."

"Yeah," said Mary Lou. "And you *liked* it. Playing that squawk, moving your shoulders like a . . . *mulatto.*"

My music wasn't perfect but it wasn't squawk, and Selda's spoons rattled like the pearly teeth of angels.

I started to shrug my shoulders, then froze, not knowing if that counted as mulatto-ish. I was aware that I was making some kind of a decision.

"Baby Girl?" Mary Lou shook her head in exasperation. "How do you expect junior cheerleaders to stay before-school friends with someone who plays with Selda?"

"Mary *Lou!*" Ellen grabbed her by the arm, pulled her so close they looked like ginger-haired Siamese twins. Her tone was harsh. "We have our *act* to think of, remember, Mary Lou? Baby Girl's unique *talent?*"

Then she smiled, sort of, at me. "We're not breaking up with you, Baby Girl. You just got to appreciate that Selda's got cooties."

Mary Lou was pouting, rubbing her arm. "To be exact,

Selda's a Peeping Tom. Even been caught by the police. Not to mention she let a relative boy *do* something to her."

A window peeker! So that's who had been at my window! All this time, Selda's hobby—

"So! Look for a refrigerator box," Ellen cheerfully instructed me. "Drag it on home when you find one."

I shook my head just a tiny bit, knowing that I was no way going to do such a thing.

Mary Lou jerked Ellen by the arm, and they walked away arguing sky high.

I knew I should have told them right then and there I'd be doing my own act for the talent show. I even had the creepy feeling it would go further: that it would be me and Selda together up on that stage. I knew it was both what I wanted and what I feared.

If such a thing came to pass, whatever progress I'd made at Cot High would dissolve quick as green Jell-O. And leave me with the same bitter aftertaste.

Saturday after that, my cat Starch had a squeaker that just about gave me a heart attack. It had to do with the dangers of his being deaf. Down Flowers Street, between Dr. Lander's Medical Clinic and the hardware store, was an open lot where building lumber was stacked. Sheriff Brasher said later that it was a hoodlum's deliberate cigarette that had started the fire. Anyhow, before we knew what was happening, we heard the Cot Volunteer Fire Department truck come wailing out of the station. Me and

Momma ran up front and peered through the window at the commotion. We were just in time to see Starch step off the sidewalk and into the street. He was the only one this side of the Mighty Mississip' who didn't hear that little red engine shrieking up our block! He folded over on the warm pavement and rolled back and forth, smiling his cat smile, like he was alone on a quiet beach.

It just happened that Dempster was wearing a flapping blue sweater that day, its center patterned bright red and yellow. I thought it was Superman—Superboy at the least—who'd swooped down to save my darling pet! That's how fast he was, and how brave! Me and Momma set to screaming: the truck flashing by, Starch rolling around, Dempster leaping in front of the truck. We feared they both were goners. Instead, what we had in the end was one hero and one living, sweet-as-pie, deaf white cat.

Momma hugged Dempster, and so did I till I realized I was squeezing the neck of a fellow classmate! A boy! I quick let go, instead thanking him from the bottom of my heart. We took him inside to reward him with frosted graham crackers and cold milk.

I cuddled Starch over on the Murphy. Momma sat at the little table with Dempster, looking deep into his innocent goldy-brown eyes. She chatted with him about how his tap dance class at Artie's was going, asked him what he did in his spare time. I could see she had that mothering feeling for him. I'd had it too, first time I saw him.

Then for some strange reason I remembered back to the first day of school in the girls' room with Selda. How she blinked her yellow eyes in the heavy drifts of cigarette smoke and warned me guys were snakes.

It was true that up until now guys in my life—my dad, Charlie Fescue and his friends, even Elvis—had let me down.

But—maybe it was because I was sitting smack on top of Aunt Lubmilla's pillow—something about Dempster felt more like the future than the past.

CHAPTER 12

A Noble Beast

Naturally I talked to Momma about Selda. No way I could associate with a person of such talent and not share it with her. Then one day Momma passed by school and saw us practicing. When I got home, she was sewing, of course. We'd made part of the front more like a living room, with an old divan, two chairs, a rag rug and a big wooden radio. Momma was set on making it pleasant for her clients, and of course at night the two of us liked to sit up there and hear the radio programs.

I plopped down on the ladder-backed chair, held my shoulders straight the way Stanley taught me and started practicing on my accordion. Starch leaped up and wedged behind my neck. He was purring and clawing me at the same time.

Momma said, "Baby Girl, was that your friend Selda? The real tall girl?" She cocked her naturally perfect brows at me. I nodded, not missing a squeeze. "Well, isn't she just exotic! All those barrettes! That's fine you two have the world of music in common."

I grinned and pumped in a heartfelt way. At my lessons, Stanley said I was getting the basics real good and the next thing down the road for me would be style. I thought, thanks to Selda, I might be getting some!

Because we didn't have real walls in our shop and grown-ups will say anything when kids are out of sight, I got to hear some interesting facts.

It was either Helen Llewellen or Loolie Llewellen—I couldn't tell the Cousins' moms apart—who said Dempster was slight because of being born too early.

"He wasn't ready," she whispered to Momma. "Only inside the womb for seven and one half months."

I could imagine her shaking her head. I remembered the womb real well, and it seemed a crime to have to leave it early. Wasn't it just like his mother to push him out first chance she got?

I was in the kitchen, lying on the Murphy bed, listening in on them, nodding my head along with the client, when Momma surprised me.

"That's not so early he won't overcome it." She spoke with real authority. "Babies come when they're ready. Dempster looks as ready a child as I've ever seen."

Helen—or Loolie—didn't say a thing. A case of a bursted bubble, was what I thought.

Momma said, "Besides, haven't you noticed his hands and feet? Just since we've been here, they've turned big. Boys and puppies grow into their feet, you know."

"How do you know so much about it?" The voice was peeved. "You a nurse wherever it is you used to come from?"

"Mmm, no, just experience . . . and keeping my eyes peeled."

"If your eyeballs are so peeled, maybe you know your girl's keeping company with that mulatto."

"Yes, that's something I know about."

"Well."

It was all said real quiet, not a single harsh word. I'd figured out that sometimes that's the way ladies fight.

My desk was dead center in homeroom, allowing me to see quite a lot of what was going on with kids inside the secret coves of their desks. Dempster sat on the side of the room near the coat closet. He whittled on that pearwood stick he'd started in the cafeteria, hands working down near his lap like they had eyes of their own. It was definitely a flute he was carving. Once he cut himself so bad, he had to use the spare gym socks he was carrying to get the bleeding stopped. He didn't fuss in the least, just doctored himself down where the teacher couldn't see.

Once he'd shaped the wood, he sandpapered it while he listened to lessons, answered questions, acted like he didn't have a sawdust factory going on between the shelter of his knees.

Off to the side in front of me was a way older boy everyone called Gumbo. He'd had some sickness when he was a baby that left him with more gums than teeth, and very little sense. He scrabbled around inside his pants half the time, everyone acting like they didn't see.

Selda sat on the other side of the room by the windows. She spent her time looking out towards freedom, not even pretending she was listening. Somehow she didn't seem to miss much anyway. If a smarty-britches blew spitballs into her braids, which looked like a crop of black hollyhocks, she didn't even have to look around to know who did it. Later, out in the hall, she'd be on him, beat him up right in front of the other boys. Guys hate getting beat by a girl worse than poison, and it kept her problems with them way down.

The everyday looks she gave guys made me think she suspected they were all up to no good. Like she said, snakes. Because of this, I believed Dempster was real brave to do what he did.

One lunch hour he brought his flute outside to where we were playing. It was finished, all polished and full of details. He held it in front of him like a white flag. That's when I noticed for myself that certain parts of him were suddenly outsized: nose, chin, Adam's apple. He kept his ears pinned down with a baseball cap, but I could tell they were humdingers. I'm sorry to say he *was* looking like Howdy Doody, just like the Cousins said.

Selda jerked her head up at the invasion. She had a way of widening her nostrils and snorting like a bull. The muscles in her neck swole up.

"You lookin' to get killed, Dumpster-Boy?"

I'd been killed before, and called bad names, and I didn't feel good about her threatening Dempster that way. The boy who'd saved Starch's life!

"Don't, Selda. Let's don't be mean."

"I *am* mean."

Her neckerchief like to cut her own throat in two.

Dempster's eyes got even bigger and wetter, but they didn't overflow. He backed away from us, tucking his flute inside his jacket like he was protecting a baby.

Next day on my way home from school, he came running after me. His in-between looks, only parts of him grown big, made me uneasy.

I said, "What now?"

"You know Selda? She peeked in my window last night. Do you think she wants to kill me the way she was saying?"

"She's looked in my window before, it don't mean a thing."

By now I'd heard from a lot of people how Selda was famous for just standing outside, staring in people's windows like she was looking for something.

"I know it doesn't, I'm not afraid, but why does she feel like that? About me? How can I make her let me play music with you two?"

I saw he wanted to real bad. But I knew if she had a mind to keep him out from under our larch, that was it.

"I doubt you can."

We stopped, both of us.

"Selda's my best friend," I said, as if speaking the words made it so. As if us playing music together, never saying an outside word, was enough for friendship. I hadn't even known till the words came out that I wanted Selda for my friend.

I looked Dempster right in the eye.

"Don't you be getting on her nerves."

Sometimes my voice has a fierceness I don't intend.

He reared his head back like I'd slapped him. I saw getting on anyone's nerves was the last thing he wanted. And hurting his feelings was the last thing *I* wanted. I owed him a *lot* for saving my cat. The whole predicament—Selda on one end, Dempster on the other—yanked at my heart. I turned away and walked high-speed for home.

Dempster went right on ahead standing close to us the next few days. Selda glowered, the rhythm of her spoons going deliberately crazy. Then one day she amazed us all by jutting her chin at him, meaning he could step in, play his flute with us. She refused to follow his music, though, and he had to play like Hades to keep up.

I think he surprised her, the way he took off on that flute—the pearwood tones warm as gold, the playing bold and loose.

It was clear to both of us: his music was perfectly wonderful.

After that, leave it to me to be the excited one.

First thing next day, I said, "Does everyone vote to be a band? I'd really like us to be a band, and if everyone does, we could do the talent show, win us a trip of a lifetime to ElfLand, raise your hand if you want to."

Dempster's hand shot right up, but Selda said, "What's so great about ElfLand?"

"*Amusement*, Selda, something we all could use."

She looked off to the horizon, but her long arm drifted toward the sky like she had an invisible balloon tied to it.

We had us a band!

She sighed. "I s'pose next we got the problem of naming ourselves."

"Drawing from a hat's the way to go about it." I snatched off Dempster's baseball cap, and I swear his ears went *proing*.

"Okay." I fished a pencil stub and a torn napkin out of my pocket. "Each writes down their choice of band name, and then *Selda* gets to draw 'cause she started it."

I was so roused, I'd turned bossy.

Selda said, "If I started it, I get to name it. What I want is the Gangsters."

I shook my head. "It has to be a drawing." This was the first time I dared cross Selda in any way. "But you can be the one to reach in."

She bashed the ground with the heel of her boot.

I passed the pencil around and we took turns hunched over little scraps of paper, printing our choices in secret.

I shuffled the papers around and stood back, motioned to Selda. Real quick she plucked one out, unfolded it.

She rolled her eyes, balled the paper up, threw it on the ground.

Dempster picked it back up and read it. His brown eyes turned shiny as a beer bottle. I knew he'd won even before he made the announcement.

"Our band will be known as the Gerbils."

Selda cursed.

I wasn't too crazy for the name either. I'd wanted "the Fabulettes," but I said, "We have to stick with it, Selda, no matter if we've gotten named after a large-faced mouse."

Dempster said, "I *have* a gerbil, gerbils are noble beasts that can jump *feet* into the air and go almost forever without water, a thing no person in the world can do! And at least it doesn't perform crimes on people or kill them like gangsters do!"

He was so passionate, I couldn't help but nod.

Selda made her snorting noise and kicked at an old tabby cat that was eating out of the schoolyard trash bin. Luckily, it was on to her and leaped the fence just in time.

Dempster and I held our breath, fearing Selda's temper, fearing someone who'd kick a cat. But nothing came of it, and in the end she was fair and let us stay with the name.

CHAPTER 13

Dead in Bed

Dempster's mother eventually found out about our band and stormed straight over to Momma's shop. I was taking a hot bath in back and heard everything.

She said, "What kind of mother are you? To let your girl keep company with Selda? Don't you know three-four years ago she *murdered* somebody? And worse than that, she's a Peeping Tom!"

The murder surprised me, but not as much as my momma's mild answer.

Momma's voice dropped low so I knew something not intended for my ears was coming. By sitting very still in the tub, I caught every word.

"What I heard was her cousin raped her. What I heard was that same cousin died a natural death in his sleep two weeks later."

The room went quiet as ice.

My mother spoke again, using the same firm, hushed voice. "Guess that makes more sense than how a little girl twelve years old could up and kill a full-grown boy age of seventeen."

A chair scraped the floor, and beyond that the bell jingled: another client coming in.

Dempster's mother said, "You and that girl of yours got some nerve coming into Cot acting like you can read the future *and the past!*"

She slammed out so hard the bell didn't make a sound. I knew it had flipped upside down; I'd seen that happen before.

It was quiet for a few seconds, and then I heard the voice of the town's librarian. Miss Flora. Fawna's grown daughter.

She said, "I'm glad Baby Girl's befriended Selda. Most people don't know what that family has been through. Her mother—have you met Patsy? Well, she supports them all on her own. I can appreciate that. My mother did it all alone, the same as you do too. Patsy's done very well for herself. A house and a car. It all comes from her book royalties."

"I heard she was a writer. Love stories, is it?"

"Mmm, romances, as far as any of us knows. Patsy uses a pseudonym. We're all in the dark which books are hers. For all I know, the library's full of them!"

This was no more a surprise to me than if Miss Flora said Selda's mother was a salamander. That's how much Selda talked about things.

By the time Miss Flora left and I heard Momma lock up, the hot water had turned my feet pink as sliced watermelon. I flipped little waves with them, thinking about how Momma knew more things than I thought. More things than I did, that's for sure.

I climbed out, leaving puddles of water as I wandered through the velveteen middle room to the front, wanting to find out about rape and how it was a boy could drop dead in his sleep.

"Baby Girl, you're getting too old to traipse around in the nude like that. Put on your robe and wipe up all that water. And remind me to buy you a brassiere next time we're in Centerville."

I looked down at myself. The cool air on my wet skin had brought my nipples out! There they were, like the heads of little pink turtles! The more I stared, the more I could see the way I had puffed up; boobies were on the way.

"Okay, Momma."

I went back for a towel. I didn't really want to know those other things anyway, about rape and dead boys. They were for sure troublesome subjects. Else why would the grown-ups have been whispering?

At first I didn't think much about Stanley Lemon starting to come all the way over to Cot to give me lessons, because I just didn't. But when my mother remarked how obliging such a thing was, I could see it was so. *Mighty* obliging.

I'd heard the story from his brother Artie, the way Stanley's wife had come down with the blues, wasted off to nothing and finally died sitting in their car in the garage. Too wasted, I guess, to even turn it off. Another person that had dropped dead—just like Selda's cousin.

It slid through my mind that maybe I'd take a step forward in making a friendship with Selda, ask her about some of the things I'd been hearing.

"You know much about rape, Selda? Or folks dropping dead in their sleep?"

Her eyes about popped out. "You *messing* with me, Baby Girl?"

Maybe I should have edged into things a little slower. She was quite a bit different than Beverly or Madeline or Penny, and she punished me for not paying attention to that. For one full week she kept her back turned to me and her spoons in her pocket.

Friends, parents, people of all kinds remained a mystery to me. I decided to keep my questions to myself.

It was right around then I saw my first crime in Cot. Me and Selda and Dempster had been given permission to go out after dark, attend a musical performance in the basement of St. Edith's Church. Gospel Willy had come to town. He was old, Negro, and world-famous. Cot's churchgoers had invited him here to sing.

The three of us left St. Edith's ready to die and go to heaven, he'd made it sound so good. Even the most stiff-mannered of the ladies tipped their shoulders back and forth to his music, and a few blurted out "Hallelujah!"

Gospel Willy *jammed* with that squally old voice of his. Wheezes and spit flew from his harmonica, and he about knocked the skin off his tambourine.

We were walking home in silence, the music replaying in our heads, when we heard a crashing come from over at the town hall. There was one of those late confabs going on inside, all the town officials meeting with the mayor. Mr. Mylo's car was parked away from the streetlight, a dark car in a dark shadow. Whaling away on it was a known hoodlum, a dropout who lived down near Hootchers Alley and stole things for a living.

He was smashing the windshield with a metal bar. We rushed over, thinking I don't know what, that we'd get him, haul him to the sheriff's. He just laughed a barking laugh at us, hopped on his shiny black dangerous-looking motorcycle and roared past us.

We shook our heads at the poor Lincoln, murmured that Mr. Mylo was the town's most generous man to those in need. Why his car? Me and Dempster went up the town hall steps to give the bad news to the adults inside.

Selda said "Later," and went her own way. I suspected she'd seen worse than this before. And Dempster and I knew no way would she go inside with all the bigwigs and fluorescent lights.

Sheriff Brasher said later he couldn't do a thing. Since

we were only minors our testimony didn't count. Plus the hoodlum had come up with an alibi for himself.

Still, he got what was coming. Someone sprayed his motorcycle a permanent shocking pink. Even the leather seat was thick with pink paint. The bike now looked like it belonged to Debbie Reynolds. It must've gotten to him, 'cause next thing we knew, he'd moved over to Tuber Valley and Cot was crime-free again.

I wondered if maybe some sheriff's deputy had taken the law in his own hands. I liked the idea of a lawman having a sense of humor.

As Momma put it, Stanley was a peach to spend time driving to our house for lessons.

She once told him, "Giving to my Baby Girl is the same as giving to me, Stanley. I'm real touched."

That led to his insisting on donating the lessons themselves.

To help repay him for his generosity, Momma asked me would I do his future.

Course I was glad to.

I led the way to my tight little room, and he shouldered in between its draped walls. His broad handsome face was tight with nerves, his normally steady eyes flittering like moth wings as they gazed at the flame of my storm candle.

He stuttered, "W-will there ever be true—you know—love, in the future? My own true love?"

I was already going dark, his question no more to me than howdy do.

110

Where I went was comfortable as being tucked into the back of the coupe, getting driven through the night to safety. It was always the same in there. Little by little a glow came from inside me and lit the future. Once in a while I'd have rather stayed inside myself, looked around for the missing chapter titled "Baby Girl." Instead I always got down to business.

Sometimes the future was shy and I had to be like a librarian, knowing just where to look. Other times the pages flapped like kids raising their hands, they were so eager to be read.

Stanley's future rocked into view. It had way more action than I'd expected, for Stanley. Someone had him on the ground, beating on him. I hadn't glimpsed anything like that since Dempster's mom and Coach Bilbo! Momma was also there, hollering her head off!

This was a shock, and in the end all I could stammer out was, *"Be careful of coaches."* Then as an afterthought, "My momma's there, in the future with you."

Just as I was getting back to normal, I blurted out, "Chocolate pie!"

This happened a lot and didn't mean much. I always came to half-starved.

For someone who'd just got a warning, Stanley seemed awful tickled. "You say your mom was there? In my future?" He thanked me over and over.

He went back up front and told my momma what a swell girl I was. They smiled at each other like there was no tomorrow, and Momma wedged out Fudge Parfait pie for all of us. Life was so nice here at home, I like to popped.

My accordion lessons were on Wednesday nights. After instructions Stanley and I took turns playing polkas and dancing with Momma. I guess Artie heard the fun, because he started coming down too. Wednesday was the only night except Sunday he didn't give dance classes, so it worked out perfect.

The two brothers were full of music, but when it came to talking, they hardly had a single word for each other. It was like they saved everything for Momma.

Then, for some reason, Stanley switched my lessons to Thursday nights, and it was back to the three of us again.

Right off the bat, the first Thursday lesson, he brought Momma a pound of chocolate-covered raisins. And for me, a tissue-wrapped charm bracelet! Not so many silver doodads as Cozy Strickland's, but a real fine start.

I examined the three charms: a little cat, a musical note and a fat little heart you could put pictures into.

"Oh, Stanley!" Momma fastened it on me. "You thought out each and every one!"

"Yes." He ducked his head. "I did."

I gave him a hug and it felt real nice. A rough tweed man-coat, big strong arms, the smell of pipe tobacco—nothing scary about him!

I left the two of them beaming at each other and went to search out old snapshots. I cut out a tiny picture of me that

Momma had taken when we were on our escape trip. My face was round and smiling with true relief. I couldn't find one of Momma in the right size, so for now, it was just my own head I carried around in the locket.

Tuesday evenings the library stayed open late. It was so close, Momma let me walk there by myself. I loved that, crossing patches of streetlight, patches of dark, two different worlds on one sidewalk.

The library was overfull of books, but tidy as Miss Flora herself. I had two favorite sections: Music and Fantasy. Though I had begun to add in Romances.

"Good evening, Baby Girl," Miss Flora said. "I've got *The Science of Music* set aside for you. It's slightly ahead of your reading level, but it's good for you to stretch your abilities."

I looked at all the small type, no illustrations even on the cover. Was this something I could do? I surprised myself by nodding. "I suspect this'll be just fine."

"*Ex*-pect. You mean you anticipate. *Sus*-pect means distrust. Doubt."

I looked up at her, wondering if she was making fun of me.

"I know you're excellent at spelling, Baby Girl. But you need to work on your grammar and diction. You're a bright girl. A lot of kids from school will stay in Cot all their lives. Someone like you should consider college. Travel." Her eyes were kind and no-nonsense at the same time. "Outside Cot, you'll be judged by how you speak."

"Oh."

"And pay attention to syntax—the arrangement of words—in the books you read. A few of your teachers speak well; listen to them. Listen to yourself."

She smiled, making what she'd said seem not so embarrassing.

I said, "OK." Then, "I mean *all right* . . . two words, two 'l's."

Her smile was suddenly dazzling; if she'd had on a wig, she would have looked like Fawna. "We also just got in a new Young Adult romance, *Midnight Love on Campus*." She handed it to me and winked. "Racy."

I blushed at the night scene on the cover: a girl and boy kissing under the shadow of a big tree, the windows of a dormitory lit behind them. In one window a girl, I'm guessing the roommate, watched with her hand pressed to her mouth.

"Thank you, Miss Flora."

I couldn't wait to pull down the Murphy and start reading it. I was heading out the door when I heard the *slap-tap slap-tap* of Cozy's footsteps hurrying down the steps from the Reference Section.

"Mind waiting up for me, Baby Girl?" she called.

Mind! I suspected—*ex*-pected—that anyone would be thrilled to walk next to the nicest girl in Cot!

We pushed out the door, and I walked slow so she could keep up. My cat Starch had followed me to the library. He wound himself back and forth between our legs, happy to see me again.

Cozy said, "I saw you do the standing broad jump in

your gym class this morning. You have real talent in those legs, Baby Girl."

"Thank you, Cozy." I knew how it was not to have something everyone else had. "And you've got a real swell speaking voice."

I reached to pick up Starch. It would be the worst, if he tripped Cozy.

In that second, something whizzed right over my head. It landed with the worst kind of thunk in the world: something terrible heavy, hitting a human being in the noggin.

Just that quick, there was poor Cozy, lying flat on her back. She was knocked out, a savage gash across her forehead.

The remains of a shattered whiskey jug glittered in her hair and all down the sidewalk.

The reek of whiskey mixed with blood, the wrongness of Cozy collapsed there, put me in shock.

I hardly remember the rest. They say I got Miss Flora, and Miss Flora got Dr. Lander. Cozy was taken by ambulance to the hospital in Tuber Valley and pronounced touch-and-go. Dr. Lander called in Sheriff Brasher.

He asked me questions, but I didn't know a thing more than he did. He scratched his head and said it was one of two things: done on purpose—but who the heck would hurt Cozy?—or done by accident.

"What about your Sight, young lady?" The sheriff pointed a finger at the words on our storefront. "The way it says right there?"

I could only shake my head and hope he wouldn't arrest

me for false advertisements. Lately my Sight wasn't worth two beans.

It was Starch who more likely knew the answer. He hid under the Murphy for two days solid.

Then came another shock. One Saturday me and Momma came back from Centerville. We'd had BLTs at Woolworth's, bought a few new bolts of taffeta, and a double-A brassiere, fitted to me by an expert saleslady. Afterwards we stopped by Lemon's Shoe Store.

Stanley whispered, "You bring your instrument?"

Of course I *had* brought it, I took it everywhere. By the time I scooted out to the car and back with it, he had taken his own down from the wall and strapped it on.

Right there in front of his customers, me and Stanley—Stanley and I—played a loud duet. He was getting plain outgoing!

Later, in private, he told me I was getting what I most hoped for: *style!*

Back in Cot, Artie was waiting for us in front of the shop with news, his lank body almost tap-dancing with eagerness.

"Your landlady came through from where you used to live. Plump, with frizzy gray hair? She was on her way to ElfLand and drove past your sign. She said the thought came to her, 'How many Bettinas do I know that sew dresses?' and she flipped a U-ie and came back. I heard her knocking on your door and came down.

"She said, 'Is this the Bettina with a hearty-built girl?' and I said *yes ma'am!*"

Momma and I had quit breathing.

Artie lifted his sloped red eyebrows, expecting something more from us.

"She recollected you both fondly and said she understood why you didn't take the time to say goodbye. She's going to write, invite you two back for a good long visit."

I hardly noticed that Artie's eyebrows were about to fly off his forehead. My mind was locked on how I'd rather chew caterpillars than take up the landlady's invitation to visit anywhere near her house.

"Anyhoo! She left a message." His eyes unfocused like he was reading off the inside of his skull.

" 'Tell Bettina the trailer blew up last month at two in the A.M.,' she said. 'Wouldn't a certain someone be for sure in bed at that hour?'

"Next morning she looked down through binoculars: nothing left but smithereens. She said, 'Anyone that would have been in bed, would be dead.' " Artie's words whistled with excitement. "She called the police and they said fine by them. Then she said, 'Tell Bettina she's free and clear.' " Artie's eyes tumbled back into place.

Momma and I reached to squeeze hands.

Artie cocked his head. "I didn't know that, about you living in a trailer. They can be real nice inside."

"Curiosity killed the cat," I croaked.

Momma led me into the shop and locked the door. Artie stood on the other side of the glass a minute, looking crushed. I pulled the shade down.

We stayed inside until Monday, hardly saying boo to each other all Saturday evening, getting used to the idea of being free and clear. Sunday we had kind of a party, celebrating Momma being a genuine widow. We fixed up bowls of meat chili and ice cream and invited Artie down to patch things up.

He tossed his hat on top of the hundred-pound meat grinder we'd never been able to either budge or make look like anything but a butcher shop leftover. The hat gave it some style and made me and Momma laugh.

Artie laughed too, then gave us the good news that Cozy was finally back home from the hospital. She had a part-time headache and a scar that would need covering up with bangs, but she'd made it.

He told us Sheriff Brasher had gone looking to Selda for clues.

Artie spoke in the sheriff's voice: "Selda, you're always on the street even though you oughtn't be, so let me ask you pointblank, did you see who heaved that whiskey bottle, barely missing Baby Girl and knocking Cozy to Kingdom Come?"

Artie shook his head, taking on the role of Selda.

"You can't help me out one little bit on this, Selda?" is what the sheriff supposedly said. "Was it maybe some boozer from Hootchers Alley? Or that hoodlum with the pink cycle?"

"I wasn't patrolling the library that night," Selda said. "I had been, I'd've put things right."

"That's the kind of thinking gets you in trouble, Miss High and Mighty."

"It was *you* came to *me*, Sheriff." That was Selda okay, unfazed by adults even if they were the law. Finally she added, "I can tell you all the bullies, Charlie Fescue and them, they were home when it happened. More likely it was an undesirable, just passing through."

Artie shook his head, recalling it. He repeated *undesirable*, then hooted.

Me and Momma shrugged at each other, not getting his drift.

He choked back honks of laughter. "It's *Selda* most people would call undesirable."

I frowned, hoping Artie's humor didn't have a mean streak to it, the way my dad's had.

Momma used her sternest voice. "Now, Artie, Selda's Baby Girl's good friend."

"Sorry," he mumbled, and blushed to his roots. "Anyhoo. The upshot is Cozy's going to be fine, and Sheriff Brasher's declared the whole thing an accident."

Hearing that set me to playing Momma's all-time favorite tune, "Roll Out the Barrel." My music had punch to it. It spoke for me.

Artie grinned, wagging his head to the beat. He was in heaven, being there with us.

I was in heaven too.

Way back, when Stanley asked me why I desired to play the accordion, I'd written down my deepest desire:

I wish to get back what my dead father stole from me.

Calling Dad dead back then was only a wish. I'd yearned for it, same way I yearned for a voice.

Momma's and Artie's faces went wide as I paused, drew

a mighty breath and *ooff*ed together the sides of my accordion. A booming, gleeful, splinter-sided note quaked through the shop, down the alley and over the roofs of town. I imagined it circling the clouds, tugging the fierce ears of Aunt Lubmilla's 'venging angel.

She'd know what it meant: all my wishes come true.

CHAPTER 14

Fine by Me

That branchy schoolyard larch was good as any roof, and me and Selda and Dempster practiced under it rain or shine. Momma made me a padded rainproof holder for my accordion, so I could take it outside in safety. She'd affixed a silver star to the carrier, which tells you she thought I was going places.

The Cot High student body didn't feel that way. Not a practice went by that someone didn't shout, "Squeak, squeak, I hear a pack of Gerbils."

Or, "Look what fell out of the larch—a whole nest of oddballs."

Like that was funny.

Cozy, as usual, was the exception.

She limped over one day, her hair in a new longer style,

covering up her poor scar. She said, "You kids are coming along! Don't listen to the others. They're just being smart alecks."

I stared at the neatly combed hairdo and the older way she dressed. Her earnest eyes and round face made her look wise as an owl. It was like she'd already grown up inside. I wondered if that was a side effect of suffering from polio.

Dempster said, "Cozy, you're the greatest. Cot wouldn't be Cot without you."

Selda nodded her head once—more of an upward jerk of her fine strong jaw—which we took for agreement.

Cozy beamed like she had no idea. I was proud of Dempster for saying what was in all our hearts.

It wasn't that long away till spring and the talent show, but I still hadn't told the Cousins I wouldn't be calling out the future for their act. I'd had too many shocks lately, and didn't look forward to the wicked chewing-out I knew they'd give me for quitting them.

They kept on picking me up, but I was back to walking behind them. The only time they turned to talk to me was to give directions about what I was supposed to do for the act: sit real still, call out the answers real loud, be painting the refrigerator box—that they thought I'd found but hadn't—in a certain shrill pattern of colors.

I saw I didn't really have a thing in common with the Cousins. I didn't much even care whether they were my before-school friends or not. My music and the Gerbils were enough for me.

Every day I vowed I'd tell Mary Lou and Ellen I wouldn't be doing an act with them. And every day I didn't.

It was still cold enough weather that I had to wear heavy clothes outside to practice. So did Dempster, who seemed to be a different-looking, different-sized, different-voiced person every week.

But Selda wore sleeveless shirts, showing off arm muscles that rippled to the crash of her spoons. Her fingernails were painted blood-red and were long and curved as claws.

One day she surprised me by asking me to her house. It was the first proof I had she saw us as friends. It turned out to be a regular house with a regular white-skinned mother: plump, soft-spoken and real nice.

"This is Patsy," was all Selda said. Leaving it to me to figure out Patsy was her mother. Not even introducing her as Mrs. Someone.

"Nice to meet you, . . ." Patsy looked at Selda for help.

"Baby Girl," I said.

"Nice to meet . . . a baby girl," she finished. She gave me a gentle, confused smile.

Selda's room was all pink and ruffly. She looked so out of place, her tough jerky way of moving, pointing with her chin, her muscles against the satin coverlet, it made me feel . . . dizzy.

She sat on her canopy bed and bounced a tangerine on the palm of her hand. Tangerines being both her Number One favorite fruit and her favorite color.

One time at school she took a tangerine out of her shirt pocket and just stared at it.

I said, "That looks real good, Selda."

"Yeah, it's good." She'd been in a mood. "Good for choking down someone's throat."

Today was another story. She peeled the fruit with her thumbnail, delicately unscrewed it in one long spice-smelling piece, fed me sweet little sections like I was her baby bird.

My friend was really something. A surprise a minute.

I stared at her profile. Her jaw was strong and sharp, her face set forward in an unusual way. Like she used it to hatchet her way through life. Even her shoulder blades were sharp, sprouted like wings under her thin tangerine-colored shirt.

She pulled off her boots and socks, a shocking thing she'd never done before. She had beautiful feet with pale undersides and perfect long toes. She'd polished the rounded toenails a completely different color than her blood-red fingertips. They were the soft blameless pink of the inside of a seashell or a baby's ear.

She tucked her feet under her when she saw me looking.

Right next to her bed was her own portable record player. She put on a scratchy record. It was Gospel Willy singing about getting to heaven. Selda did her spoons, *clickity click*, right along with him. The music was as spooky in that fluffy room as Selda herself.

I gazed at a mirrored shelf lined with a row of Barbies I couldn't imagine she'd ever played with. And that's when I spied it! Displayed right there in the middle was a tall can of spray paint, its cap a telltale shocking pink.

My mind flashed to the hoodlum bashing Mr. Mylo's car. The pink vengeance done to his motorcycle.

Except for her music, I had no idea what went on in Selda's head.

I said I had to go home. Selda just nodded and kept agitating her spoons. I wandered through the modern-style rooms, making my way to the front door. The living room was empty. From off in the kitchen came the small noises of tidying up. Opening onto the living room was a little office with a desk and typewriter. I looked in. There were two stacks of typed pages on the desk, looking ready to go. Two big manila envelopes addressed to Blue Book Press.

I peered over to see the title page. *Horny Hot Humps Hilda*, it said. By Roscoe Ryder.

My eyes like to come out their sockets! I'd heard from kids what humping meant! Did this mean Selda's sweet-voiced soft-bodied mother was Roscoe Ryder? Who wrote about *humping*? Somehow I knew it did.

I leaned as far into the room as I could without stepping

125

in. Like this wasn't the same as snooping. The second stack was titled *Rubylips Raptures Reverend Roy*.

My heart was banging like fury. These weren't the titles of romance stories! Romances were called *Storms of the Heart* and *Kiss of the Masked Crusader*. And they were about women named Lady Rosamonde, not Rubylips!

I backed away from the stories like they were coiled snakes, jumped when Patsy called from the kitchen, "Would you girls care for Fig Newtons?"

"No!" Selda shouted from her room like she'd been offered worm pie. I skeedaddled out the front door.

Next morning before school, I tracked down Dempster, found him sorting out his locker. It was filled with juggling balls, carving supplies, sheet music and the library books *First Aid for Gerbils* and *Ten Easy Lessons to Kick Boxing*.

"You ever been to Selda's house?" I asked.

He smiled a crookedy smile. His features were still awkward, but his jaw had lengthened and his body was filling out, making him look stronger and more like other guys.

He nodded and said, "Once," in a meaningful way. "I was assigned to tutor Selda. Except it turned out she already knew everything."

The words *Roscoe Ryder* shimmied in the air between us, even though I had no way of knowing how much Dempster knew.

I swear he read my mind.

"It's hard having no husband to help out." Sometimes he said things an old person would say. I wondered if this came from having an elderly dad. "Your mom's lucky she has her talent for dresses."

I nodded. It *was* lucky about Momma, and that we had the old Singer.

After that, it was like me and Dempster—Dempster and I—shared a secret. In some ways, although I kept it from Selda, I felt more like it was Dempster who was my best friend.

Mary Lou had been staring at Dempster and me having lunch in the cafeteria. Before we went out to practice, she pulled me aside and said in a real sly voice, "You and Dempster going steady?"

"No!"

"Oh, I wondered."

"We're not."

"He's turning out real cute, now that he's taller than me."

I recognized that look. She was about to ask a favor.

"I was thinking, since you two are both Gerbils, could you ask him would he like to go with me?"

I don't know why that irritated me so bad—so bad*ly*. "He can't," I said. "His mother won't allow it." That much was probably true.

"Well then, see if he's in my future."

"He's not." I hurried off to catch up with Dempster.

"Hey!" Mary Lou yelled. "You didn't even go into a trance! You didn't lose the Sight, did you? You'd better not! Don't you goof up me and El's act!"

I caught up with Dempster and hauled him through the double doors to the schoolyard, which he seemed to think was real funny.

CHAPTER 15

Questions Are Popped

Third report card, I brought my grades up from three A's, one C and one F (math), to four A's and one B. It seemed like learning my way around the accordion had opened my eyes to arithmetic, my formerly complete worst subject. I had hardly any tardies this time and even my grammar was better: a big X right in the *Shows Improvement* box!

My momma about fell over with pride.

Then she took my stocky hands in her slim ones and said she had big news for me too.

"Stanley and I are getting married this spring, Baby Girl! We're going to be one happy family!"

It was my turn to about fall over. Momma and I hugged real hard, but that night in bed, I held a flashlight up to my face and looked in the mirror, the way I always do when I need to cry. A flood of tears burst out. My face went from flat to puffy in about ten seconds. I tried to do it quietly, but Momma heard me from the front room. She came back to the Murphy, took one look at my splotchy cheeks and cried right along with me.

"Don't you worry, honey, this won't be anything the same as before." She brought a cool washrag to clean me up. "Stanley's just crazy for you, he's even moving to Cot, starting up a second shoe store here just so you don't have to change schools, you're doing so good."

I was nodding, wanting so much for it to be true.

"I'm ugly, Momma."

"Oh, Baby Girl, you're not! You're always saying I'm so pretty and you're going to end up with the very same face. And you've got that nice sturdy frame, not an old bird-bone like me."

"They say I'm fat, Momma—"

"You're *strong*, Baby Girl. And in proportion." Her eyes were welling up again. "Besides, everyone goes through stages, it's real hard to know what you'll look like in a few years. I don't even know what *I'll* look like—probably all toothless and gray-headed!"

A few hiccups of laughter broke out of us and we mopped our eyes.

Momma sighed. "Stanley was going to tell you, but we want you and your friends to play at the wedding. After the vows, that is. You'll be my bridesmaid, so we'll use a record for the walk-in—"

"Even Selda?" I was remembering the other day and how she'd knocked a tooth out of Gumbo's mouth when he tried to rub against her. I couldn't imagine her at such a serious and important occasion.

"Of course, honey, Selda's your special good friend. And Dempster's invited. All the Gerbils. See, Baby Girl? It's going to be fine."

I didn't dare look over at the back windows with Momma in the room. The pairs of panes were black and shiny as eyes, the sheer curtains no more use than see-through lids. I had the strong feeling Selda was back there in the alley, taking in the sight. I guess that's the way it is with friends, wanting to know every little thing about each other.

The next day Selda offered some of her few words to me. "You got it made."

I waited for how it was I did.

"Having a pretty mother like that, giving you love and passing on her looks. Getting to live like you do. Velvet walls. Taking baths in the kitchen and getting to sleep there too. Everything 'cept for those 'pugnant cats slithering round your back door."

She'd never been inside our shop. She wouldn't even come in for cinnamon toast and hardly said boo to my momma. It seemed like she didn't even care I knew she'd been peeping.

"Your mom seems to give you love too, Selda. And you've got a real nice house. I'd just kill to have myself a fine canopy bed like yours. Momma and I hope to have a house ourselves, in the future."

"Huh. You don't get it, how our lives are different and are going to *stay* different." She was frowning. She got peeved so easy. "'Sides, what do you know about killing?"

"I get the ways we're the *same,* Selda. Nice moms, both of us playing instruments. Not having dads."

"I *have* a dad, he just don't come around. For all I know, I'm his spitting image."

"My dad's dead. He looked like a walrus."

"Yeah, well."

I got used to the idea of the wedding real quickly, specially after Stanley drove over the next day and took us by a big house up on Starlight Drive.

He said, "I'm fixing to buy this house for us, based on your two's approval. That big upstairs bedroom?" He pointed to the corner of the house, wrapped in the arms of some kind of fine tree, just on the edge of blossoming out. Tall windows peeked through the twigs. They looked out over town but no one could look back in. "It would be yours alone, Baby Girl, unless you want Starch coming in to share it."

That was nice, his knowing Starch by name. "Fine by me."

Momma stared at the creamy white paint, the snazzy columns holding up the porch, like she was seeing heaven.

"Oh, *Stanley.*"

She folded me in her arms and we looked up at our real

and future home. When she leaned us back against Stanley's chest, I felt through her bones that she'd been weary for a real long time.

Stanley stood there like a planted oak tree, the weight of me and Momma no bother to him at all.

Stanley drove us home. He barely got out his car door when Artie flew down the steps.

"I heard the rotten news, Brother, how you've stolen Bettina right out from under me!"

He knocked Stanley to the ground and started whaling on him. They were silent as rolling logs, nothing but the gruesome sound of slugging each other.

Momma screamed bloody murder and pulled me out of the way, but I kept on watching.

Stanley flipped on top, cracked his brother on the jaw and knocked him cold. He carried him limp up to the dance studio.

"Sorry, Bettina," Stanley muttered. "I feared it'd come to this."

"Oh, Stanley . . ." Momma had a beat-down look on her face, something I hadn't seen since the trailer days.

I was hopping around, all stirred up, remembering I'd already seen this in Stanley's future. I was real glad he hadn't gotten killed. At least not before the wedding. I was set on having that upstairs bedroom.

For everything that happened good, something happened bad.

A few days later, dropped through the mail slot along with the bills came a handwritten envelope with our old landlady's name on the return. It was a small square card-sized envelope. Hefty. I didn't need my Sight to guess that the invitation to visit her had arrived. Eager exclamation marks were drawn like bombs all over the back, and the stiff flap was dangerously open at one corner. Just looking at it was like getting paper cuts on my eyes.

What Dad had said was true: the landlady was a Buttinski with a capital "B"!

But that was the only thing my dad was right about. He would never be dead enough for me to take one step towards the landlady's executive ranch-style house, with its picture window view of the burnt remains of a trailer and a father.

Telling myself I was sparing Momma trouble, I took the letter straight out the back door. I intended to put it in one of the garbage cans at the end of the alley, but a few steps out I froze. There in the shadows were Ellen Llewellen and Rooster Kaminski! I could tell by their silhouettes: Ellen's womanly chest, Rooster's spiky hairdo.

He was mashing his leg between hers and had his hands wedged up under her tight sweater. Seemed like he was trying to choke her large bosoms to death. He was huffing and she was moaning, and the whole sight made me feel faint.

They were so caught up in what they were doing, they didn't even see me. I stepped back inside. It was confusing.

I'd just seen Carline in the halls wearing Rooster's letter sweater. Meaning they were one step away from engagement—and now here he was with Ellen.

Momma called back from the storefront, "We get the mail yet, Baby Girl?"

I startled, pushed the unopened letter to the bottom of my panties drawer, leaving things of the past sealed inside.

Wasn't it just like the landlady to jump to conclusions? To think we'd be in some big hurry to go visit her, or collect up my father's bone ash? I'd had it with bone ash.

No matter what, I didn't plan to go back where we'd come from!

Word got around about the wedding and the house on Starlight Drive. How things were moving up for us. When clients ordered Apricot Ball gowns for their teen girls, they asked Momma over for tea. Dempster's mom even came by, all sweetness and cream, wanting to make up.

"Call me Winnie. And I'll call you Bettina without the Miss."

She told Momma she'd like to give her a wedding shower, "when the time comes."

They sat there and chatted, Winnie in a straw hat and a sun-colored linen suit that set off big golden brown eyes that were so like Dempster's.

I'd crept into my velveteen room so I could peek out, listen without them knowing. As usual, I found out a few things. Momma told Winnie she planned to keep our shop going. She'd be hiring help for the afternoons so she could be home, fix her family proper dinners.

Fine by me, I thought. Imagining beef stew boiling on top of a big white six-burner. Me doing homework at the kitchen table, Stanley helping with the answers.

Winnie said, "You know, Bettina, our kids are real good friends, and I'm glad of that—but what do you think of them playing tunes with that Selda?" Before Momma had a chance to say, Winnie tried to put ideas in her mind. "Don't you think we should put a stop to it? 'Fore there's a scandal?"

"No, Winnie," Momma said. "I do not."

"But Selda—"

"She's the leader of the band, I saw that from the get-go. What she's doing is offering our kids a musical experience. That's Culture, Winnie, with a capital C."

Winnie chewed on that. "I do want Dempster getting his full share of culture."

"And you know about Selda's mother? She's a real author, maybe even has books in the library."

"I'll be! You ever met my husband, Earl? Retired from owning hardware stores? Well, he reads books."

I leaned forward and my chair creaked heavily. Winnie's voice snapped off like a broken twig. It'd be a miracle if they didn't catch on I was spying.

"Anyway," she finally said. "Maybe after graduation, our kids'll go off to Tuber State together. I can't decide if Dempster should do business or lawyering. You know which brings in the most?"

"Hmm. No, I don't."

"Oh." She went quiet, thinking it over. "You fixed on a major for Baby Girl yet?"

"No, Winnie, I haven't. I 'spect she'll figure out her own future. Right now we're just concentrating on her growing up some."

"Mmm . . . better not wait too long, do you think?"

I was shocked by talk of college. Was I supposed to be planning ahead? I had no idea what my future would be! My Sight was a failure when it came to me. My main concerns were getting through the talent contest and perfecting my new style of doing pushups.

Later, when I was fixing tuna on Ry-Krisp for me and Starch, Momma called back, "Listening in's the same as being sneaky . . . you aware of that, Baby Girl?"

"Yes, Momma."

"All right, then."

It was like the Lemon brothers had changed one into the other. Gap-toothed Artie grew solemn and hardly ever smiled anymore. Everyone said he'd taken it hard that Momma had left him for Stanley. I hadn't even known she was with Artie.

I asked her and she said, "No, Baby Girl. It's news to me, too. A crying shame he saw it like that."

He was so miserable to be around, I quit my dance lessons altogether. We could hear him turning mean upstairs, something we'd never have believed could happen. Some folks even said he'd taken to drink.

137

Once we heard him shout at Dempster, "No! Tap, step-step, tap, *half*-turn—no, *no*! You're hopeless!"

Dempster's size had made him a little awkward.

We listened as he fled down the steps, sobbing, and we shook our heads. He was a real sensitive boy.

Then somebody deliberately kicked over our trash can and we had to scoop coffee grounds and tomato scraps back inside.

Momma said, "I'm not saying it was Artie did this, but it has got to stop."

But she feared another fight, and didn't say a word to Stanley.

Stanley had meantime turned all smiles and was every bit the charmer Artie had once been. He'd bought himself a snazzy new accordion, bright black and decorated with rhinestones. We had a whole set of old-timey duets we did together, Momma smiling and clapping along.

She was looking young enough to be my sister, rosy-cheeked, pale hair bouncing with waves.

Once the engagement was official, an aunt of the Lemon brothers came from Centerville to visit us. If she knew about Artie's bad behavior, she never said a word. She got directly to questions no one else had dared to ask us.

Where exactly did we come from, who had my father been, what had my momma's father done for a living?

Momma folded her hands in her lap. She was ready for her.

"Mrs. Lemon—I believe I'll save calling you Aunt Lura until after the ceremony—Baby Girl and I believe sorrows of the past should be borne in private. We wouldn't think of burdening a sensitive lady like yourself on this pleasant occasion."

"Well." Aunt Lura's eyes wiggled, not sure if she'd been praised or insulted.

I wondered if Momma had used a mirror to practice those words, in the way I used one to cry.

She was my momma, I was with her most all the time, but she carried mysteries my Sight couldn't see into. I hoped I would be like her when I grew up, have my own share of mystery.

I did the future for Aunt Lura before she left, but it was just words. "You were named by a family member. You have one or more favorite hats. You have a reputation for delicious fruitcake."

She admired my picture of Jesus pinned to the curtain, and on the way out said to my mother, "How does she do it? Aren't you proud?"

"Mmm," Momma said.

The bell tinkled, I snapped down the shade and locked the door. Momma and I rolled our eyes at each other.

That evening we had a supper of the leftover goodies we'd served Aunt Lura. Everything cozy until Momma said, "Honey, I been wanting to talk to you about something."

I breathed in the crumbs of a peanut butter cookie and like to choked.

I figured she'd caught Selda peeking in or seen her bash one of the kids in a street fight. It didn't occur to me I might be the one in Dutch.

"On the Teen Talent Show?" she said.

I nodded.

"Well, can you be in more than one act?"

I shook my head, started chewing my thumbnail.

"I know you're practicing real hard on your accordion, made yourself up a band and everything, but one of my clients was mentioning you were doing a magic act with Mary Lou and Ellen. . . ."

It was a question. I nodded, gnawing my nail to the quick.

"Are you leading someone on, Baby Girl?"

I burst into tears. "Yes, Momma, I am."

"Well, I guess you have some straightening out to do 'fore this gets any farther down the pike."

She patted my hand, counting on me to do the right thing.

That really set me to bawling.

Next morning I woke up dreading what I had to do. When the Cousins came up the block, I was outside, ready to declare my intentions.

"Hey, Baby Girl!" Mary Lou was in one of her friendly moods. "What do you think of having a little window in your cardboard box, and you'd stick your head through to yell out the answers, and you'd be wearing some kind of *monster mask*? To, you know, keep the mystery of who you are?"

That took the cake. That was no way the kind of mystery I wanted for myself.

Ellen didn't say anything. She was in that half-smiling daydreamy state she'd been stuck in for the last month. I swear her breasts looked bigger than watermelons today. Maybe they seemed so big because I'd just gotten dressed myself, tucked my own little pair inside their tidy brassiere.

We were almost to school when I blurted it out. "I'm not going to be in your act."

There was a moment of shocked silence.

"I knew it!" cried Mary Lou. "You've lost the Sight, haven't you? If you ever had it at all!"

"I have my own act. The Gerbils and I . . ."

We'd stopped in front of Carline and Rooster, who were holding hands. Rooster dropped hands and stood there gawking at Ellen's chest.

Someone muttered slyly, "Ellen is swellin' . . . again," which made me think I hadn't been imagining how huge she'd gotten.

"Carline!" Mary Lou screeched. "Can you *believe* this? Baby Girl's gone and lost the Sight, just when we were counting on her for our act—"

Carline frowned. "She got *my* future right. I'm coming up to be Miss Apricot and—" She nudged Rooster with her elbow, and he jumped. "—And she was right as rain about me and Rooster's future, married and business tycoons over at ElfLand—"

Ellen came out of her trance and turned on me. "What about *my* future with Rooster—"

The bell rang and I bolted through the school doors and up the stairs to homeroom. Where Rooster kicked my desk from behind the whole period.

Chapter 16

'N' More

My Sight seemed to be getting everyone in trouble. Including me. All the confidence my music had built up turned backward on me: I developed the heebie-jeebies. They would come and go, but I was always left feeling crawly under the skin.

I confided this to Selda.

She shrugged a sharp shoulder. "I was born jumping out my skin."

"How come, Selda? You got a nice house and all."

"World's full of trouble. Somebody's got to be ready."

"Oh." I'd never thought about it that way. "That why you keep an eye on things? At night?"

"Hmpf."

I'd been hoping for something more from her. Advice. "So how do I get rid of feeling so nerve-wracked?"

She shook her head, meaning I couldn't. "Trick's in not lettin' on."

My Sight never told me a thing about what the future would bring me, but my momma did. My chest was developing just like she'd said it would. I was almost fourteen, and Momma said it was time to talk about my monthlies. Momma told me she'd started hers when she was fourteen. I'd heard things whispered in code, girlfriend to girl-friend: periods that had nothing to do with sentences; the curse; being on rags. But the only girlfriend I had didn't whisper her secrets to me. Like I was about a lot of parts of growing up, I was in the dark.

Momma's talk started, "Not all cycles have two wheels and pedals, Baby Girl."

The whole notion of bleeding into pads got me in a mood. I felt put out with her, like it was a scheme kept se-cret from me. But from what she was saying, there was not a thing I could do about it.

No doubt the Cousins had theirs already. Mary Lou was still flat in the chest—it was like everything went into that butt of hers—but from the size of Ellen's breasts, I figured she must have started her monthlies in grade school.

I wasn't walking with them anymore, of course, not since we'd had words, so I was slow to notice Ellen hadn't been to school in a while. Then, when I had to leave homeroom to go to the bathroom, I saw her mother (*Loolie* Llewellen?

Helen Llewellen?) down the hall, cleaning out Ellen's locker. She was working with real fast, jerky moves, stuffing everything into a pillowcase. When I passed her, she looked up and frowned in a way that meant don't say a word.

I didn't. I practically tiptoed past. I hate to be in Dutch with anyone. But soon as school was out, I found Mary Lou.

"Is Ellen sick?"

"I thought you could see everything! Or did you really lose your Sight, Miss Smarty-pants?"

She was still sore as a hen about my not agreeing to be in the cardboard box. "You playing dumb, Baby Girl, or you really don't know?"

I shook my head.

"She got sent to Tuber Valley. Our mothers are forcing her to stay with our meanest strictest worst aunt and uncle till everything's over. . . ."

I frowned.

"Where are you from? Mars? You said it yourself—'Ellen plus Rooster equals love 'n' more.' Well, it's the 'more' that got her."

"Rooster . . . ?"

"Yes, stupid! She's P.G." She was practically shouting.

I saw Dempster out the edge of my eye, coming to my rescue.

"Why didn't you warn her!" Mary Lou cried.

Dempster moved between us like a referee. I turned blindly to reach for his hand, but Mary Lou had beat me to it.

Her voice turned to sugar. She was talking to him but looking at me. "Come on, Dempsty, buy me another of those chocolate Cokes?"

Dempsty? He shrugged at me and smiled. I looked at them with new eyes: how pretty Mary Lou was, her thick ginger hair and pouty smile. The long slender torso that made being small up top look desirable. And Dempster had grown shoulders and was inches taller than she was. His features matched up perfectly now, the long-lashed eyes and good straight golden-brown hair. Even his ears looked normal. Fairly.

Mary Lou tugged on his hand and got him headed for the door.

That quick they were gone: my new worst enemy and the best of my two best friends.

CHAPTER 17

The Monthly Blues

That night Stanley picked up Momma for a date at Captain Carl's C-Food over in Tuber Valley. I knew, after the sad and shocking day I'd had, that being alone at home would send me to the mirror for a red-faced cry. It was already gnawing on me, what had happened to Ellen Llewellen. She was the slightly nicer of the two cousins; at least *she'd* never gone after Dempster.

Could I have done anything to help her from getting in such a fix?

My conscience was starting to get to me. I pulled on Momma's best sweater, stretching it out a little, and sneaked out through the alley. Artie'd turned so spiteful, I knew he'd tell if he saw me.

I walked over to Selda's, crept through her backyard—

something I'd usually never do in a million years—and looked in at her. There she stood, wearing only the bottoms of her pj's, gazing in the mirror and playing the spoons to that same rusty old tune on the record. She had a way of dancing without hardly moving, like she was wound so tight she danced from the inside out. Her head tucked back with each beat, like the waves of music slapped her soft in the face.

Her flat round breasts seemed like just two more muscles on her chest. Watching her, I got a strange pitching in my stomach.

She turned her slow yellow eyes and looked straight through the window at me. Like she'd been waiting for me to show up. Heebie-jeebies zigged up and down my spine. It was as if I was Selda and she was me.

She shrugged into a denim work shirt and came outside.

"Fag?" She tamped a Lucky on the pack, ready to light it for herself.

"Sure. I'll take a half."

She broke hers in two, lit both at the same time and put one piece in my mouth. I sucked, chest clenched to keep myself from coughing.

I think I'd finally surprised her.

She gave me her first smile, a smile so sweet it turned her into some kind of braid-headed angel. For that second, it took the strangeness out of her, and let me completely love her.

We stood there in the middle of the chilly yard, fire-flies of ash streaking the dark. The Lucky was horrible but I stayed with it, then ground it into the stiff grass like a pro.

"Bye, Selda."

"Bye, Baby Girl."

By pure bad luck Momma put on that same sweater the next night, sniffed a bagged-out sleeve and said, "P.U."

She looked at me real hard. I studied my social studies book like my life depended on it.

Her silent questions hung there in the air between us, so loud they broke me.

I looked up and said, *"What?"* in my most peeved voice.

Momma arched her brows, shucked the sweater back off and soaked it in a sink full of Woolite.

That was the start of me taking things out on Momma that weren't her fault. Like how my body seemed unlikely to grow tall and leggy like Carline Halsey or the Cousins. And how the fuzz on my legs was a shade darker now and you couldn't help but notice it.

Momma showed me how to use the electric shaver.

She said, "It's just for legs, Baby Girl. Don't take it to your arms. That's no more than silver peach fuzz, and shaving would turn it to bristle."

The legs came out good, but not getting to do the arms just made me mad at her all over again.

And my face, which Momma said was pretty as Shirley Temple's, was not. She plucked my heavy gold eyebrows, which I admit did help, but I resented her suggestion that I wash my face with Noxzema. As if I didn't have enough to do, without having to tend a complexion!

With the coming of spring, all the flowers and sunshine worsened my mood. Too many things were happening. Everyone talking about the Apricot Ball, me with no date for it, the Gerbils getting ready for the talent show, Momma's wedding just around the corner.

Life was getting too rushed and too complicated.

Then my monthlies arrived! I kept throwing my panties away and pretending nothing was happening until I flat ran out of underwear. In the end, Momma caught on and got me fitted with stanching supplies. I worried that everyone could tell, but Momma said no, they couldn't.

On top of that, the Gerbils weren't coming along as good—as *well*—as before either. I just couldn't get in jive with Dempster's flute.

Selda said, "What's the matter with you, Baby Girl? Get with it."

"It's not her fault," Dempster said. "I'm adding in too many notes."

Selda stared at him and shook her head.

I stared at him too. He'd taken out his juggling balls and was doing a routine that involved whirling between tosses and *kicking* the balls back up in the air. He could kick his leg nearly over his head! That's how he was, always real quietly working on something, always coming up with things I'd never think of.

I guess I was lucky we still played as a band and I had an

hour every day under the larch with him. The rest of the time he'd become Mary Lou's. She had a lock hold on him, pulling him around the halls like he was a first prize she'd won.

She was lonesome without Ellen, I knew that, but I had some real hateful feelings for her anyway.

At home, I had the sense ghosts prowled our alleyway, but each time I checked there was nothing. I guess it was the memory of Ellen and Rooster pressed against each other that haunted me. It made me want to do what they were doing, and at the same time made me feel scared about what could happen. Ellen had gotten P.G.! The worst thing that could happen at Cot High! Or maybe anywhere!

A lot of my time was spent daydreaming about how it would be, to be with a boy. One recent change was I'd finally gotten rid of Charlie, that creep, as costar of my private thoughts. There wasn't even an audition. Just one day, the new person I was dreaming about was Dempster.

Whenever I was alone, I read over and over the chapter in my health textbook called "After the Wedding." It was like a hobby, finding out what things interested my body.

This led to not paying strict attention at school, and the grades on my tests began to slip back down.

I started pouting about doing the future for clients.

"Fine," Momma said. "Your Sight's a gift, not a punishment. Do what you like."

Her not forcing me made me decide to do them after all. Though sometimes I'd say cruel things to the ladies, like

"There will be more babies" or "Your husband prefers a small waist," bringing tears to their eyes.

Even though I wasn't growing much, I was too large for any of Momma's clothes or shoes, or even her hats.

When she made me hats of my own, I wouldn't wear them.

The nicer she was, the more hateful I was back.

"Oh, Baby Girl, let's not quarrel, you're breaking my heart!"

"I hate that name, Baby Girl, it's not even a name, I hate it, it's *embarrassing!*"

"Well, honey, I didn't know that. You've just always been my Baby Girl. We can change it. What would you like? Suzette? Lucille?"

"Forget it." Then after a minute, "*Mary Lou* is what I wanted and now it's already taken."

Momma nodded and kept stitching, finishing up my beautiful pearl-crusted sky-blue satin bridesmaid dress.

CHAPTER 18

---❦---

Starlight Drive

I sneaked out again, this time while Momma was still at home. She had scads of Apricot Ball gowns to finish up there in the front room, and worked late every night. It was a relief, her not having as much time to notice me.

Although I didn't plan it, I ended up walking all the way through town and up the steep road to Starlight Drive. I guess I was hankering to see our future house again, like it could set me free from the present.

Above town, the air was black, and sharp with pine. Without a light-stealing moon, the stars multiplied and snapped like bold white eyes. I gazed overhead, hoping for something like a guardian angel. Instead, the stars shifted in a peculiar way, moved in for a closer look at me.

Below the ridge spread the lights of town, a Technicolor reflection of the sky. Walking up that winding road, lights glittering above and below, put me in a trance. It was like floating through the Milky Way.

At the top of Starlight Drive, the landscape turned swank. Houses here were separated by trees and land. Lawns rolled forward like bolts of sumptuous cloth, and wicked-looking concrete elves, pale as knucklebones, crouched along curved driveways.

I walked by one of the smaller houses, a super-tidy place. Instead of trees it had square bushes up both sides of a walk that led straight to the front door.

All around the house were spotlights shining against the walls, like the bricks were on display.

And there, right in a beam of light, was Selda! Standing bold as brass, looking in one of the side windows!

With a small crash, the window flew open and a guy jumped out right in Selda's face.

"Cut it out, Selda!" he said. "You're really ticking me off, doing this. Quit it or I'm voting you out of the Gerbils!"

Dempster! I swear on a Bible I'd forgotten he lived on Starlight. If I'd ever known it at all.

Selda said, "Ha, I *am* the Gerbils." But she backed off from him and loped across the front lawn, headed straight for me.

"You stealing my scene, Baby Girl? Cot don't need but one window peeker and that's *me*."

Dempster peered into the dark. "Baby Girl? Is that you?"

Selda snorted. "You two are a *pair*! A pair of gerbils is what I'm thinking."

She pawed the ground with the heavy boots she always wore, even with dresses, then took off running fast as the Olympics.

Dempster called after her, "Be careful! Charlie's gang is out tonight, it's basketball practice."

Through the darkness, we heard her distant snort.

Dempster turned to me. "Hey."

"Hey." Being alone with Dempster in the dark made me shy. "How come she has to be careful of Charlie?"

"Oh, you know . . . those guys talk about doing things to Selda. 'Cause of what happened to her before. Makes them want it to happen again."

Dempster made his voice cheerful and changed the subject. "You up having a look at your new house?"

Leave it to him to know.

We walked real slow. Four houses down, we turned in at the Sold sign, and sat on the dark porch steps. Its deep stone arms made a fort around us.

Dempster was wearing a soft plaid flannel shirt with a pocket that suddenly squeaked and bulged. A little gerbil head, cute as the dickens, popped up.

Dempster took it out real gently. "Meet Prince Valiant."

Prince Valiant had fur so soft and thick, it was nothing short of coat-quality. He had huge eyes, a long nude tail and a solemn oversized head that

155

reminded me of our landlord, Mr. Mylo. His smell was a cross between cedar and feet. He looked at me with googly black eyes and wiggled his whiskers. It wasn't so bad, having a band named after something this cute! I held him in the crook of my neck and let him root around in my hair.

Dempster gazed at me like I was sugar. He reached to put his little pet in an empty packing box, but his eyes never left my face.

Just that minute, across the valley, a full moon rolled above the hills. We stared. It was too big, too strangely colored to be a regular moon. A tangerine moon is what it was, swollen and quilted, its light erasing stars as it rose. Something powerful built in the air. Without seeming to move, our shoulders were touching. The feel of this boy burned me clear through my blouse. We looked full at each other and time stopped short.

"Dempster." It was more a breath than a word.

He put his hand on my cheek, moving my face just a little closer to his. "I love your voice," he murmured, " . . . whispery and blue as a storm cloud."

And then we were in a heart-stopping, blood-connecting, never-ending kiss.

By the time we finally finished, I was in love.

We tried another one, and it turned overwhelming. We held each other tight, pushed against each other's mouths like we hoped to get swallowed up. It scared us both, what we felt was so big.

We stood up, like that was a remedy, but Dempster was still pressed against me in a way I couldn't help but like. We had to break away again or . . . I don't know what!

We tucked Prince Valiant back in Dempster's pocket and walked hand in hand down the hill. Dempster saw me all the way home like I was too precious to take chances with. We pushed right in the front door, Dempster still holding my hand.

Momma looked startled. As far as she knew, I was still in the back working on algebra!

She arranged her mind around what she was seeing and smiled at us.

"Glad to see you, Dempster. 'Fraid I'm knee-deep in Apricot gowns, but you two go on back and make up a snack."

"Gowns. Apricots." Dempster was nodding. "That's all Mary Lou talks about."

Momma said, "That doesn't surprise me. It's a real big occasion and something on every girl's mind."

Dempster tilted his head like this was news. "Are apricots and dancing something of interest to you, Baby Girl? I mean, we could go if you'd want to?"

I almost said what about Mary Lou, but suddenly that didn't matter. I knew this much: real girlfriends got taken to Apricot Balls; plain friends never made it past chocolate Cokes.

"Yes." I tried tucking my smile in a little. "I'd want to go."

"Okay then."

He was smiling back his own beautiful smile. I could see clear as day the man coming out in him.

"I've got to get home; Mother doesn't even know I'm gone. She thinks it's swell you-all are moving into that big white house. Be our new neighbors."

Neighbors! Wasn't life seeming perfect!

"Bye, Miss Bettina. Bye, Baby Girl."

The bell clanged and he was gone.

Momma said, "Wade through this mess of chiffon and give me a hug, honeybunch."

It was one of those long hugs, ending in a sigh that did all the talking for us.

That night was the beginning of taking long baths in the dark. Momma never came back to interrupt me and never questioned the habit. Even though she didn't hear any rough singing or splashing around in the tub. Two things I'd always done.

Floating in that warm water, I was a mermaid, nothing to distract me from the feel of my body. Respecting its fine health instead of griping over its looks was a sign of how I was getting along better with myself. I appreciated the smoothness of the strong muscles of my legs and hips. Ribs that were beginning to surface. The pleasant soft-hardness of new breasts. Long blond hair that drifted around my shoulders like silver seaweed.

———

At practice the next day, things were normal as pie. It was like Selda had never even seen us the night before. She led off with a hot-paced medley Dempster had named "Rocket." We'd made it up specially for the talent show and aimed for it to last the full three minutes allowed.

CHAPTER 19

More Fun than Monkeys

I decided to wear my sky-blue bridesmaid dress to the Apricot Ball. It was already stitched together and only needed last-minute adjustments. It was okay with Momma if I wore it the one time before her wedding.

The adjustments were in the right direction: easing the seams through the bust, taking several good tucks in at the waist.

"Baby Girl, you've got a real nice figure on you!" Momma said through a mouthful of pins. "Just like I always said."

I smiled, looking at myself in the mirror. Big shapely legs that could broad jump. Smooth wide shoulders, just meant to squeeze an accordion.

No wonder Mary Lou had started looking daggers at me, every time I passed by with her ex.

It was a real formal occasion, the night of the ball. Stanley came over early from Centerville, not wanting to miss me all dressed up. He wore a suit and sat in the front room with Momma, fidgeting and nodding to her chatter.

Dempster came to the door in a tuxedo he'd rented from us. Just seeing him set my heart to going. He pinned a corsage next to my bosom.

Momma said, "An orchid! You must have special-ordered it from Tuber!"

"Don't you two look"—Stanley cleared his throat—"shipshape." He nodded in relief at finding a word.

Dempster's dad just sat out in his car, waiting. Momma waved for him to come on in.

He flung open the Pontiac door and eagerly toddled inside. He was very old for a dad.

"Well, hello, folks! Just call me Earl." He was ready with a joke. "On account of that's my name!"

"That's a good one, Mr. Earl," Stanley said.

Fortunately, Earl did enough laughing for both of them.

Despite Earl's high spirits, he looked a mite frail. The shape of his head showed through his hair, and his thin hands were peckered with brown spots. The top half of him was dressed in a bow tie and shiny jacket, but the bottom half was in pajamas and slippers. I guess he figured he'd only be seen driving the car. Nobody made a point of it.

Stanley shook hands with him, Momma did the conversation and Dempster and I just stood there stiff as boards, rolling our eyes at each other.

We sat in the back of the sedan like Dempster's dad was the chauffeur. When we pulled up to the school gymnasium, we saw every one was arriving like that: fathers in front, kids in back.

Except for a few kids who had their own jalopies. Like good old Charlie Fescue, who pulled right up in front of us, giving us a clear view of his date—Mary Lou. He stepped out, yellow hair slicked back in a ducktail, broad jaw and shoulders, pale hooded eyes looking for trouble— like some kind of belligerent god. He thumped the top of his car, meaning for Mary Lou to get out. You could see it was a struggle for her to do it on her own. She kicked open the door with a high heel, gathered up her skirts with her hands and pushed her way out. I almost felt sorry for her.

Crawling out from the backseat came their double dates, Rooster and Carline. It seemed a little disloyal for Mary Lou to double with the boy who'd gotten her cousin P.G., but I wasn't up on all the rules of behavior.

Carline was of course dressed perfect—perfectly—for being Miss Apricot. She wore the fabulous apricot satin dress Momma had designed for her, and even had a tiara pressed into her beauty-shop curls.

She was the most beautiful girl in school, no doubt of that. She could have been a movie star.

I swear I don't know what she saw in Rooster, his red hair sticking up like he'd had a fright, and a sneer that had permanently wrecked his mouth.

I asked Selda once, if the reason why both girls liked Rooster was because he was big and had muscles to spare.

She snorted and said she'd seen the muscle that made him so popular—with girls that were nothing but *hens*.

I nodded. I understood what she meant, but I couldn't understand how such a thing would make him more likable.

Mary Lou was wearing pointy satin spike heels. She teetered along behind Charlie until she finally caught him by the arm. She glared over her shoulder and straight into the backseat window of our car. I glanced at Dempster, who was suddenly busy adjusting the buttons on his tuxedo.

Inside, the gym was bright and rowdy. Miss Flora and her friend, school nurse Bonnie Bivens, sat at a table up front. I noticed how pretty they were, in a grown-up way, and that they'd managed to make it fun, counting the Miss Apricot votes. But what caught my attention was the I.Q. shining out their eyes, something rare here in Cot. I was captivated by it. Maybe I *would* find myself a major, go off to college like they had. . . .

They gave me and Dempster—Dempster and me—ballots to X in for Miss Apricot. I didn't even glance at mine. I didn't feel like voting in a contest that wasn't a contest. Besides, Carline had been rude to me and to my momma.

When I turned around, Dempster was looking at me real close, in that way he had. "You look so pretty, Baby Girl."

I suspected it was the shiny bridesmaid dress that had him dazzled, but I was glad he said it.

"You too."

We headed for the punch bowl.

Fawna was head volunteer chaperone. She was back to wearing her blond wig and was dressed to kill in a black sheath. Her ears dangled with rhinestone clip-ons. She sure had a nice figure for someone with wrinkles and a librarian-aged daughter.

She dipped out cups of purple drink for us. "Aren't you two a match made in heaven! You look plain adorable!"

We gulped down our punch, and Fawna handed us two twigs of apricot blossoms: one for my hair, one for Dempster's buttonhole. I noticed the whole room was heavy with the soft-ripe smell of apricots. I wondered if the room had been sprayed with something, or if the heated-up girls were giving off the scent. I knew they couldn't *really* be apricots, the way the school motto said. I sneak-tasted my forearm anyway and was relieved to find it regular-salty.

Thanks to our lessons, both of us knew dance steps. We lit right into a routine. Dempster was fast and loose, just like Artie, and he had me off the ground so much of the time I felt like one of his juggling balls. I swear, we were having more fun than monkeys! We were so good at the lindy hop, kids made a circle around us, cheering when Dempster flung me between his legs and caught me on the other side!

Then the lights went low and mirrored balls shot sparkles through the air in a glamorous and dreamy way. A swell record came on, a slow one with lots of falsetto. We danced slower and slower. We were hardly moving, just holding tight. Light sprinkled over us like pixie dust, and all I could think was *love 'n' more*.

I couldn't imagine there'd be a better moment in my life.

Then the lights rudely snapped on and a lot of murmuring and rearranging of the crowd took place. A certain few girls were led to the stage. Three of them in all, arranged behind the principal. Carline was in the middle, looking the very picture of an Apricot beauty queen.

The principal's hearty voice boomed over the microphone.

"And now, boys and girls, what we've all been waiting for. The votes are tallied and we have a brand-new Miss Apricot!"

A few girls in the crowd squealed.

He opened the envelope too close to the microphone and it crackled like a firestorm across the gymnasium.

"Second runner-up is . . . Brandy Branson!" Then he squinted at the paper again, like he couldn't believe what he saw. "First runner-up is . . . Carline Halsey? Is that right?" He shook his head in genuine confusion, and went on like the rest was an afterthought. "So, according to this, our Apricot for this year . . . is . . . is Cozy Strickland."

Cozy wore different-sized ballet slippers and a long pink dress that covered her leg brace. When she limped forward everyone cheered. Real tears ran down her sweet pale moon-face. Her smile trembled.

But it was Carline I watched. Her lips had stiffened into what she must have thought was a good-sport smile, but her eyes were locked onto mine. She looked fit to kill. All her older sisters had been Apricots, and it was me who told her she would be too.

Before the ceremony was half finished, she stomped off the stage, pushed her way toward us.

The principal ogled her backside like it was the town treasure.

"Fake!" she cried. "Baby Girl, you are an outsider and a no-good fake. You've got no more Sight than a mole."

Mary Lou elbowed her way to Carline's side.

"That is so true!" she joined in. "Everything Baby Girl says is a lie! She promised to be in me and Ellen's act, and she broke her word. She stole Dempster from me. And—and—it's all her fault Ellen got P.G.!"

There was dead silence while everybody thought that one over.

The principal, for reasons unknown, had followed Carline down into the fray like a monster-sized puppy. Cozy was left on the stage without even a congratulation from him.

Under his bulging forehead, his sharky, naked eyes darted from Carline to Mary Lou.

"What the Sam Hill's going on, Carline?"

Dempster tensed at my side. I couldn't tell if it was me or the others upsetting him. He hadn't known anything about me agreeing to do an act with the Cousins, or me predicting Carline's Apricothood, or specially that Ellen's condition had to do with me. Not that it did!

I shocked everyone, especially myself, by saying in a

voice cool as my mother's, "The future's what you make of it, Carline. We get what we deserve. And Mary Lou? I think you can thank Rooster more than me for 'pregnating Ellen."

After a second, everyone burst out laughing and Mary Lou like to turned purple.

Fawna pushed by us, bound up on the stage where Cozy and Brandy were standing, arms at their sides, looking bewildered.

She grabbed the microphone and started singing real loud and cheerful, *"Here she comes, love-ly Miss A-pri-cot."*

There were whistles and shouts when she drew Cozy forward and placed the crown on top of her head.

"Way to go, Cozy!"

And "It's about time!"

Fawna hung a red cape over Cozy's shoulders, and Brandy was nice enough to press a bundle of apricot blossoms into her hands.

Dempster put his arms around me and whispered in a gangster voice, "I woulda stomped those lousy rats for ya, kid, but ya beat me to it."

I laughed, but what I felt was relief at a real bad moment passing over.

It was only afterward, when I was home in bed reliving the glories of the night, that I realized Selda hadn't come to the ball.

Of course she hadn't!

No boy I knew, except Dempster, would ever ask Selda

to a dance. It came to me that she was right: I *did* have it made, compared to her. I guess I'd known from the beginning our lives would always be different. But like Selda told me, I didn't really *get* it. Not until now.

I vowed that Monday I'd take her a tangerine to school.

Chapter 20

In Dutch

We had the usual assembly the following Monday morning. Dempster sat next to me, and from the looks we got—especially from Mary Lou—I knew it was around that we were a couple.

Selda, as usual, sat apart from me, this time down the row about a dozen seats. I passed her down a tangerine, the nicest one at the market. A boy between her and me aimed it over her head and threw it hard, but her arm shot up quicker than a rattlesnake, and she plucked it right out of the air. She leaned forward and smiled over at me.

A rare sight, and to me, precious as gold.

Everyone went silent as the principal took up the microphone.

No one in the world could have predicted the subject of his announcement. Most specially me.

He was looking all somber. "We had our fun at the Apricot Ball, and now we have to address a situation that is not quite so pleasant." He cleared his throat. "As you know, not everyone in our little town is from here."

Everyone looked around. Everyone *was* from here, except me.

"And I'm not saying that's a bad thing, this is America, differences are tolerated. But I will *not* put up with lying and fortune-telling and contributing to the downfall of at least one of our own girls. A *hometown* girl, who found herself under the influence of an outsider, and was encouraged to compromise her . . . maidenhood."

There were gasps. A word like that had never been used in assembly.

"Students have come to me with reports of broken promises, of broken hearts, and by God, *I will not have it!*"

The principal had turned into an angry red-faced preacher. He was staring straight at me, and scaring me spitless.

I hunkered down in my seat, wondering what the heck I'd done to stir up such a storm.

Dempster whispered in my ear, "Don't worry."

"Commitments have not been honored!" he roared. "An act for the Teen Talent Show has been torn asunder. I do not have the power to discipline the offender, but I can do this: in fairness to those with genuine talent, I will judge the talent show acts myself, along with two other fair and impartial citizens." He swung his arm out to the side. "Mr. Arthur Lemon? Mrs. Lorraine Halsey? Will you join me, please?"

First Artie, then Carline's grandmother appeared from behind the stage and stood on either side of the principal. All three had their feet planted and arms crossed, forming a righteous team.

A few teachers clapped weak hands.

The principal nodded. "You are a fine student body, but you are not yet adults. Votes can go astray; I saw this for myself at the Apricot Ball."

Cozy Strickland seemed to be the first one to catch his meaning. She rose with the dignity of a true Miss Apricot and limped up the aisle and out of the auditorium.

"Oh, now, oh, for heaven's sake, let's calm down here." It was satisfying, seeing the principal flustered. "*That's* not what I was getting at, we all like Cozy just fine . . . beauty isn't necessarily the point of being an Apricot . . . well, I hope some of you in the audience see the trouble you've caused! Assembly dismissed!"

The students were so riled up, the teacher herded us out to the schoolyard and told us to get hold of our horses. Dempster was swept ahead and I lost sight of him.

Carline and Mary Lou, all of a sudden best friends, were behind me. When we got to the top of the outside

171

steps, they shoved me with all their might. I fell real hard, books scattering everywhere, both my knees scraped to the bone.

Mary Lou said, "See what happens, Miss Priss Boyfriend-Stealing Faker? When you interfere with how things are *supposed* to be at Cot High?"

I felt like hitting them. I was capable of hitting them real hard. A vision scorched my eyes: me and Selda together, sending them to the hospital with broken faces. But I was already in Dutch with the principal. That was bad enough.

Instead, I turned away and hobbled over to the larch, where Dempster and Selda were already warming up.

We Gerbils had a policy of always carrying our instruments with us so we could practice during any spare moment. That was hardest for me since my accordion was so big, but I did it. When I unfastened my carrier, I saw that the fall had dented the instrument's edge.

The damage wouldn't affect the sound, but it hit me hard. The accordion, perfect for generations, and now this!

I touched the crinkled metal and blinked back tears. Dempster smoothed my cheek and made soft noises. Selda looked off toward the horizon and gave my shoulder two hard pats.

"I'm sorry." My voice was shaky. "I've wrecked things for the Gerbils. I don't know why the principal's so mad at me."

Dempster said, "He's Carline's uncle by marriage, is why."

"He's got the *hots* for Carline, you mean." Selda kicked the blameless old larch in the shins. "He's messed with ever' one of her sisters. There they'd be, sixteen years old and he's still bouncing them on his lap. I *seen* him!"

I wondered what other unimaginable sights Selda had come across, patrolling the streets at night. I said, "Well, he won't be voting for us no matter what. And neither will Artie Lemon; he's our neighbor and mad as a hornet about Momma marrying his brother."

"Selda!" Dempster's eyes were bright. "You could tell the principal what you saw him do to Carline's sisters! Then he'd have to let the audience decide the winners!"

"Huh-*unh*! I'm doing just like I always do, not saying a word. My mom wants me to graduate and it's taking me some time, but I plan to do that for her."

It was the first time I'd heard Selda show her feelings for her mom.

I said, "Let's just practice, and be the best Gerbils we can. We still have the wedding!"

Selda and Dempster nodded, and we lit into the rocket number, doing it top to bottom four times before we got herded back to class.

Nobody noticed my knees, so I went to Nurse Biven's office by myself. She sprayed me with Bactine and put on Band-Aids.

"'Preciate it, Nurse Bivens. Specially your being gentle."

"*A*-ppreciate it, Baby Girl. *Es*-pecially."

In cahoots with Miss Flora! I liked that they'd been talking about me, maybe thinking I was worthwhile.

We smiled and nodded at each other.

CHAPTER 21

———◆———

Birthdays and Broken Hearts

It was my fifteenth birthday. The time in spring when trees are full out, but their leaves are still pale, fragile and perfect. Both things reminders it had been a year since we left my father, traveled a world away.

I'd been too shy to tell Dempster it was my special day. When he hadn't guessed, it got me down in the dumps. Even though thinking he could guess such a thing didn't make a lick of sense!

Selda *had* guessed, or heard it through the kitchen windows. She bought me a true-friendship present, wrapped up pretty as a picture. She gave it to me after Gerbil practice, in private.

"Here."

It was a real silver charm from the jeweler's in

Centerville! For my collection! A flat silver eye, complete with eyelashes. On the back was engraved I.C.U.

"Thank you, Selda." I was about to bawl. "I see you too."

"Hmpf."

Stanley announced he'd be taking me and Momma out to the diner in the evening, to celebrate my birthday with burgers.

It was already dark by the time I went to the back room to dress for dinner in the special new birthday outfit Momma made me. All the while I pulled on clothes, I had a certain familiar feeling. Before I left the kitchen, I called to the windows, "See you later, Selda."

I thought I saw the bright streak of a burning cigarette flash across the panes and out of sight, but I was already pushing into the velveteen room and couldn't be sure.

It was a little embarrassing going out with Momma and Stanley. He was not quite my dad yet. He was in fact my mother's *boyfriend*.

I didn't know what the kids would think of that. For my part, I certainly didn't care to dwell on the particulars of Momma and Stanley romancing. It was my hope it was late enough that anyone from school would've gone home for supper.

The diner was busy, mostly with regulars, the farmers and widowers, tucking into the Tuesday Night Special: meat loaf, whipped potatoes, green beans and rolls; coffee and apricot pie to follow.

Fawna's fat-bellied calico cat greeted me at the door, rubbing on my leg like she'd missed me. I saw this as a good start to our night out.

The only booth left was right by the front door. I slid in without taking much notice of the others. Momma said hellos to most everyone, she was so well known by now. She paused a second before she added, "Hello, Dempster. Hello, Mary Lou."

She scooted next to me, our backs to the rest of the diners, Stanley across from us. She gave a worried look to Stanley, and reached to pat my hand.

Stanley, who's big on throat clearing, said, "I bet you'd like some tasty onion rings to go with your cheeseburger, wouldn't you, Baby Girl?" He was talking too loudly and cheerfully.

I shrugged.

Momma said, "I know I would! And a malted! We've spent enough time this year fretting over waistlines. What do you say, honeybunch?"

I didn't want to hurt their feelings. "That sounds just swell." Even I could hear my voice was flat as a pancake.

Fawna marched over, professionally flipped a pencil from out her hair—a blue-black beehive tonight—and cocked her drawn-on blue-black eyebrows.

Stanley ordered for Momma and me, then said, "Believe I'll go for the special. Looks too good to pass up."

Fawna nodded approvingly. "All the men rave on it. Gravy, catsup or both on top the meat loaf?"

"Hey, Baby Girl, Miss Bettina!" Dempster had come up

behind Fawna and was smiling at me right over her shoulder. He looked sweet and innocent as apricot pie. "Howdy, Mr. Lemon."

"Don't bother the happy family, Dempsty," said Mary Lou, suddenly at his side and dragging on him the way she always did. "We got better things to do."

"Well, bye then, see you tomorrow, Baby Girl."

Mary Lou bounced them through the door.

It was clear to everyone what was happening. Spoonful by spoonful, I was getting dropped.

No one said a word. Even Fawna was silent. She stared down at her order pad like a doctor trying to come up with a prescription.

"I'll make that malted extra thick," she mumbled, and hurried off behind the counter.

Momma all of a sudden wanted to talk about the talent show, not having a clue that thanks to the principal's grudge against me, this was now a sore spot of mine.

"Walking by school the other day? I heard some of your rocket song—and honey, I about broke out clogging right there on the sidewalk."

"Artie's one of the judges, Momma, no way the Gerbils are going to win."

Momma and Stanley snagged eyes again. "Honey, I would hope Artie is fair in his judging. That would be his duty, wouldn't it, Stanley?"

Stanley folded his bottom lip over his top lip and shook his head, like he'd given up predicting his brother.

"Momma?"

"Yes, honey?"

"I feel sick to my stomach. Can I go on home?"

She surprised me by getting firm. "Sometimes a person's got to be tough, Baby Girl. Running for home's not always the answer. Besides, a malted is known to settle stomachs, isn't that so, Stanley?"

He cleared his throat again. "I believe I've heard that a time or two."

Two against one. I gave in.

Fawna plunked the frosty metal container in front of me like it was a cure for anything. I sipped a cold strawful, looked up and smiled with pleasure. Fawna winked and left us there to go on celebrating my birthday.

At least I had my family to count on.

The middle of that night, I woke with a breaking heart. I crept out of bed, not waking Momma, felt for the hand mirror, and stepped outside. One look at myself in the dim alley light, and I was there: sobbing for everything I was worth.

With all my heart, I both hated Mary Lou and loved Dempster. I didn't understand anything—myself, Dempster, or why being in love was popular if it made you feel so miserable.

Starch, my good old white cat, pushed between my ankles. I picked him up and held him against my heart, letting his purrs soak in.

When I got through with my crying jag, I took him back to bed with me.

Momma knew. She reached over to pat me and Starch, and she didn't make me push him off the Murphy.

Maybe she should have, 'cause later that night, I rolled on top of him and bent his tail in two. He yowled his head off, and Artie banged on his floor and shouted, "Shut that cat up! I never could stand that scruffy damned thing."

The swearing ticked Momma off. She sat up in bed and yelled back at the ceiling.

"That was uncalled for, Artie Lemon, you, you . . . meanie!"

In the morning, Dempster knocked on the front door, picking me up for school. I was sitting in my velveteen room, not wanting to see him.

I called out soft to Momma, "Tell him go on."

She did, and I went on myself a few minutes later. I was stewing about how to keep the Gerbils going without letting Dempster break my heart any more.

I couldn't think of a single way to go about it, except to lay down the law. I was nervous and short-tempered as a wasp by the time I got myself under the larch.

Selda and Dempster stared at me, seeing something new in my face.

It wasn't ideal, having to spill the beans in front of Selda.

"Dempster, you broke my heart going out on me with my sworn enemy Mary Lou, who pushed me from behind and caused the dent in my accordion, and even though I want the Gerbils to keep playing music and go on to fame,

180

I cannot stay being in love with you, although I haven't figured out yet how to get out of it."

The two of them blinked like I'd been speaking the Italian language.

Then this slow, one-sided smile come over Selda's face and she turned away, shaking her head. I didn't think I cared for that.

Dempster said, "Gosh. It was just a chocolate Coke we had."

"You have to swear right now not to mention another personal thing to me if I'm going to keep being a Gerbil."

"I don't swear that, Baby Girl. Mary Lou's real friendly, she—"

I spun on my heel and walked straight across the school-yard. I was the first one inside homeroom. Not even the teacher was there yet. I dug at an old scar on my wooden desktop, a pointy-tipped valentine gone over a million times with blue ballpoint pen.

Rooster came in next, his red crew cut bristling with meanness. He kicked the back of my seat real hard, then leaned forward and said, "You should see Carline and Mary Lou's new act—they are total knockouts and ten times better than you and the Mouse Turds, and they're going to *win*."

I jerked around. "Just shut up about the Gerbils, Rooster Kaminski, you are hateful clear through."

The bell rang and I was cut off as the rest of the kids poured into class and sat down. Dempster didn't even look at me.

Somehow it didn't seem like much of a victory, drawing the line with him.

I saw Dempster a couple of times in the hall with Mary Lou after that, going to class together or him sitting on the bleachers with a few other kids, watching the junior cheerleaders' practice. In the hallways, girls swarmed around him like bees. It wasn't just because he was getting cuter every day. It was because he liked them back, never once giving anyone grief.

Except me.

Of course even though I said I wouldn't, I stayed a Gerbil, and every lunch hour we still had practice. But it wasn't the same. We knew our routines so good, it hardly showed that we were short on enthusiasm. We had three routines all together—two fast, one slow—that were perfect, and about a half dozen more were good enough. Although good enough for what, we couldn't say. All we had was the talent show, and beyond that Momma and Stanley's wedding.

I guess we figured we'd need all the tunes we could get to fill up a whole wedding, so we kept on. But Dempster's silences and his attention to other girls were a constant heartbreak for me.

Selda was unhappy too. She was the one who knew if the music was one hundred percent or not. It didn't set right with her that we weren't putting ourselves into it.

One night, instead of just looking in my back window,

she tapped real soft on the door. I went out and had a cigarette with her.

We didn't say much, just leaned against the brick wall, thinking our thoughts and puffing.

Finally Selda shook her head. "You're making a hash of things, Baby Girl."

I didn't feel too good about having my last friend come out with that.

"I *said* I was sorry about the talent show, Selda—"

"Who cares about that? Our music's turned sour on account of no one getting along."

"I can't help that, Dempster did me wrong."

"You aren't the only one can get their feelings hurt, Baby Girl. Think about that."

She threw down her cigarette, let it lie there smoldering as she slipped into the shadows, disappeared quick and graceful as the alley cats she hated so much.

Most the night, I thought about what she'd said. There was no way to tell if she was talking about her own feelings or Dempster's or someone else's. I tried to go over everything recent but couldn't come up with anything that might have hurt Selda.

It was Dempster she meant, I was pretty sure of that. But if I'd hurt him, didn't he deserve it?

I decided I'd better ask Momma.

When I woke next morning, Momma was already working up front.

I decided to take an extra bath. Anymore, it seemed like being clean, having a shining ponytail, giving my lips a little gloss with Vaseline, checking the growth of my breasts, were about as important as homework.

It was my automatic habit now to inspect the windows before getting naked. I'd never seen Selda peek in the mornings, but just in case, I liked to know if someone was watching. I stepped in the tub and was scrubbing myself with Cashmere Bouquet when Momma came back to fix me breakfast.

"Excuse me, Baby Girl, for interrupting your scrubbing. It won't be long now, you'll have the privacy a teen girl needs to have."

She smiled at me, cracked an egg in the skillet, hefted the dull old butcher knife and sawed off bread for toast. She held up a jar of marmalade and I nodded. I was eating regular again, letting my body grow into its natural style. No more Ry-Krisp for me.

I leaned back in the tub and took a breath. This was the time to ask.

"Momma?"

"Um-hmm."

"You know how I went to the dance with Dempster? Well, something happened before, got me real attached to him."

I had her attention now. I'd never said a word about my feelings for Dempster.

"What happened is we had a few kisses. They proved to be real powerful."

Momma nodded without looking at me, making it easy for me to blurt it out.

"I just plain fell in love, Momma." I felt tears welling up, saying those words out loud. I missed Dempster so badly!

"Then Mary Lou got ahold of him—you saw for yourself at the diner—and I told him that was that, and now he doesn't even look at me and . . . did I do the right thing, Momma? I feel heartsick and like my future is not going to work out right."

Momma set my breakfast on the table, dragged a chair over to the tub.

"Honey, have you talked at all to Dempster? About how he's feeling and how you're feeling? About Mary Lou?"

"I can't, Momma."

Her forehead knit up. "Maybe you can't and maybe you can. You're caught up in your own feelings, which is natural when things get rough. But when you love someone, you got to feel for them too."

I didn't expect for her to side with Selda! Or ask something hard of me. When she didn't say anything more, it began to come to me that she was right. I looked up.

She was standing there, holding a towel out for me. "You got the Sight, Baby Girl, and folks come to you to see into their future. I know you want in the worst way to see your own. But the fact is, the future's a changing thing. It's what you make of what you have."

I'd said that very same thing to Mary Lou and Carline at the dance! At the time it was nothing but words.

"Like you did, Momma? Changing our future to the good?"

She gave a small nod. I felt her power boom around the kitchen like invisible lightning! How had I missed it before! What she'd done, leaving Dad and the old life behind? That was bigger than anything my Sight could do—it was bigger than the Milky Way! She'd saved herself from misery and me from certain death, using nothing more than a strong will and her talents!

And I was Bettina's daughter! It was time I tried finding my own power.

I jumped out of the tub so fast, I pushed water over the edge.

"Can I skip breakfast, Momma? I got to get ready real fast!"

She smiled and bent down to mop up the floor. "Go on. Take a banana, eat it on the way."

I pulled on my clothes, jerked my damp hair into a ponytail and made it out to the sidewalk just as Dempster came up the block.

I walked straight to him. "I'm scared to say this, but I've got to know: what are your feelings for Mary Lou?"

He brought his eyes to me real slow. I saw his heart had backed off from me by a million miles. "I like Mary Lou, if that's what you really want to know."

It took everything not to burst out crying or run away

from him. I couldn't even tell if I loved him or hated him anymore.

He was standing stock-still, his face more serious than an old man's.

Going on with this was worse than swallowing poison. "Well then, what are your feelings for me?"

Dempster's eyes were tearing up. He was brave about pains like cutting his hand with his carving knife, but I swear he cried easier than me when his heart got hurt.

"I don't know, Baby Girl. I never had such feelings as that night on your new porch, the moon colored orange and all. But a true love doesn't just walk out on you, not even letting you give your side of the story." His wet lashes had turned into star points. "I made my feelings for you change. I can't have a real girlfriend yet, Baby Girl. It's too hard."

A terrible sound broke from my throat, a sound a person with a regular voice box probably couldn't even make. I was just crushed by what I'd caused to happen.

I blurted out, "It *is* hard! But this is harder than being run over by trains! I can't bear it, not having things like they were."

He was nodding his head, and then we let our books and instruments slide to the sidewalk and were holding on to each other for dear life. There was no way we could hold back. We both burst into tears.

We heard the first bell ringing in the distance, and pulled back to give each other's face a soft salty kiss. We looked so sorrowful and red-eyed from crying, it got us to laughing.

We had to run to school and still got into homeroom after the tardy bell. I didn't know what had just happened between us, or what would come of it. But I was pretty sure I'd taken the future and changed it around for myself.

CHAPTER 22

Teen Talent

Selda was in a real bad mood the day of the Teen Talent Show. Her top lip was swollen over the bottom one.

"You been scrapping again?" I said.

The look she gave me like to fried my hair.

I pulled a tangerine out of my purse. "Here." I'd planned to give it to her anyway.

She shoved it into a pocket.

"What do you say we go for ice cream after the last act finishes up? My treat."

She shrugged.

"You scream, I scream, we all scream for ice cream?"

As usual, I couldn't come up with a thing to tickle her funny bone.

Kids started piling backstage, clustering around tables,

putting on makeup. Corners bulged with kids struggling into costumes behind hung sheets. A few contestants memorized lines out loud or did handstands.

The principal came back and raised his hand, meaning everyone be quiet and pay attention. Everyone did.

"I have an announcement of the most heinous nature."

Uh-oh, I thought. *Now what have I done?* But it was Selda who moved off, disappearing into a ruby-black fold of stage curtain.

"Charles Fescue, Cot High's finest athlete and all-around boy teen, was viciously attacked last night."

I hoped—this was the mean streak in me—that he was dead.

"He's lying in the hospital with fractured ribs and an injury that could lead to . . . his not fathering babies."

That brought up a vision I'd rather not have had.

"The sad comment on society is that the culprit, a known criminal, might just get off scot-free." He shook his head. "The heartening side of all this is that Charles's friends will continue their act tonight, doing the best they can without their captain."

The full-blown cheerleaders went into a full-blown cheer, and all Charlie's teammates whistled.

"Good luck to the rest of you. Don't any of you worry about the Teen Talent Show going right. I'll be in the front row, seeing to it justice is done!"

The principal walked down the steps and seated himself.

Dempster pulled me aside, his face gone pale. "I heard a bad rumor that Selda got arrested last night."

"For peeking?"

He shook his head. "Worse. Mother told Dad Selda hurt someone bad—sounds like it might have been Charlie."

"You think those creeps got her? In the way you said they wanted to?"

He shrugged. "Selda's mom had to pay a lawyer to get her out of Juvenile Detention."

"But it's a rumor, right? Not for sure."

He nodded.

We found Selda off in a corner digging swearwords into the wall with her pocketknife. Dempster pointed her to the dressing area and said, "Get into your costume." When she came out, he took her spoons out of her pocket and pressed them into her hand. That she let him take these liberties made Dempster arch his eyebrows at me. It seemed, for a second, we were the parents and Selda was our unhappy little girl.

Once we were dressed in the black trousers, blousy red shirts and silver-sequined vests Momma had made for us, we stood off in the wings and watched the auditorium fill up.

The center of the front row was for the three judges: the principal, Artie, and Carline's straight-backed grandmother. They sat prim and ready, hands folded, all three pairs of shoes darkly polished and gleaming.

Cot's bigwigs—Mr. Mylo, Mayor Lynch, Widow Vanderwag, Dr. Lander's family, Sheriff Brasher—filled the rest of the front row.

Somewhere in the dark rows behind them were Momma and Stanley and Dempster's folks and Selda's mom.

We tried to watch all the acts that came before us, but it was too boring to stay with it. Especially the homemade poems read out in voices so small they didn't even make it to the microphone.

We sat on the ground and did tic-tac-toe and whispered "I Spy with My Little Eye," until a loud rockabilly record grabbed our attention.

One of Rooster Kaminski's round black eyes was decorated with a bruise, and three of Charlie's other boys were plastered with stitches and Band-Aids. On cue, they leaped into a wild gymnastic dance to the music. You could kind of tell where Charlie was missing because of the moments the guys shrugged at each other and dithered in little circles. Still, I had to admit their splits and kips through the air were pretty exciting. I could see they got to the judges, too. Little nods of their heads. Artie's musical toes tapping to the beat.

Directly after that came Carline and Mary Lou's act. It was also in the gymnastics category, even though it was really one long football cheer.

The girls wore their hair in matching flips, bangs curled under just so. Their faces were unusually bright with makeup. But what was uncommon about the act was the costumes. Carline's spangly stretch leotard was cut so far down the neck, her breasts about bounced out with every leap. And Mary Lou, who had nothing in that department, had the seat of her leotard fashioned so I swear half her bottom showed. And she wasn't even wearing tights! She made it a point to turn backward a lot, waggling her fat fanny at the judges.

I don't know what Carline's grandmother thought of that—her face didn't show a thing—but the male judges grinned like jack-o'-lanterns.

There was just one act in Unique Talent, the category where Mary Lou and Ellen had wanted me to sit in a refrigerator box giving predictions while they pranced around the stage like beauty queens.

Instead, two freshman girls did cat's cradles and other fancy string arrangements with their fingers, which no one could see.

They got just about zero applause.

The first act in the Music category was Cozy Strickland and a boy named Michael Snout, both wearing overalls and straw hats and singing a two-part song from *Oklahoma!* It had a lot of personality to it.

Then we were on, our vests jagging the light like we were made of diamonds. We'd decided that instead of announcing our names and what we planned to play, we'd yell "Rocket!" and slam right into it. All of a sudden, there wasn't even time to be scared.

After about twenty seconds, the audience started bopping their shoulders and clapping along. Then came stamping feet. A few kids jumped up and started jiving in the aisle, though the teachers put a quick stop to that.

We were loose as noodles, me and Dempster throwing our shoulders and legs around like mulattos. Selda's spoons leaped left, right, overhead, like they had a life of their own. At the end, we bowed one at a time and called out our names:

"Selda!"

"Dempster!"

"Baby Girl!" I croaked.

Then all together, *"The Gerbils!"*

We just about brought down the house, everyone chanting *Ger-bils, Ger-bils,* like it was a magic word.

Offstage, we couldn't stop grinning. Even Selda let us do some hugging on her. When Dempster and I wrapped our arms around each other, we were washed away just like the first time. Without meaning to, we kissed.

We were brought apart by kids pounding us on the back, saying how cool we'd been. If it hadn't been for that, I can't say what would have happened. I was one hundred percent in favor of going wherever that kiss was leading us to.

We were happy and so stunned with feelings, it hardly mattered when the show ended the way it did.

Morris Trull, a freckled boy with a carrying voice, got third prize for his poem, "America, God's Favorite Country."

Charlie's gang took second.

Carline and Mary Lou won the grand prize.

Momma and Stanley came backstage and told us they were proud as punch.

Then Dempster's parents arrived, followed timidly by Selda's mom, Patsy. Winnie grabbed Earl's arm and turned him to face her.

"Look who's here, honey." She rattled Patsy by the arm. "My husband here? Earl? He *reads*. He's probably read ever' one of your books."

Patsy blushed, glanced nervously at Earl.

"Kids?" Stanley did his famous throat-clearing and said, "Bettina and I have been talking it over. For our honeymoon, we want to take you fine musicians for a weekend at ElfLand."

Selda turned aside, like he wasn't talking to her.

"Based on your-all's approval," he added directly to her back.

Dempster said, "Sounds like a dream come true, doesn't it, Baby Girl? Selda?"

"Overnight?" Dempster's mom said. "Would there be strict supervision?"

His dad said, "Criminitly, Winnie, don't be such a pill. What're you going to do when they get shipped off to Ed Sullivan? I declare, that's where they're headed."

She opened her mouth, then snapped it shut again as Coach Bilbo walked by, met her eyes, looked away.

It came to me then, not so much a Sight as just I'd missed it before: that under her careful makeup, Dempster's mom was a young and pretty woman, like Momma. That she had a loose, sassy way of moving that had nothing to do with her society dresses and little hats and gloves.

Her face struggled, trying to recall what her point was.

"Well, since *you're* going, Mr. Lemon, such a reputable businessman—I'm sure it will be just hunky-dory."

Her husband nodded his wrinkly little head in approval.

Selda's mom put a plump hand on Selda's hard shoulder and said real tender, "Selda?"

Selda jerked away. "No way I'll get to go," she growled. "I'll probably be in *jail.*"

"Oh, Selda, that's all done with." Patsy's voice was soft as cloud. "It was a clear case of you protecting your honor." Then in an even lower voice, "You've just got to be a little less violent, dear . . . in defending yourself. That's all the judge was saying last night."

"Hmpf." Selda did one of her snorts. "Less violent, I'da been the one in the hospital."

Dempster's mom was talking to Stanley, but I could see she was straining to hear Patsy.

"Selda?" she called over. "Earl and me 'preciate the culture you've been giving our boy, in the form of music."

Before Selda had a chance to say something gruff, I broke in. "We Gerbils want to go on our own to the diner, don't we, Selda? Celebrate things going so good. If that's okay with the parents?"

I leaned my head briefly on Stanley's tweed shoulder, letting him know I meant him too.

Our folks said, "Fine," and trooped off the stage like old friends. They had their own plans for coffee over at our shop.

The backstage had almost cleared out when Rooster stalked over, neck jutting with every step.

It was Selda he spoke to. "Don't think you're getting away with this, you half-breed freak. We're going to do you, every one of us. You don't have a chance. And when you start bawling for mercy, you're getting *none*."

I was just sizing things up, thinking between me and Selda and Dempster—who was nearly as big as Rooster—we could show Rooster what for. But the principal was still there and we'd get kicked out of school and—

Before Rooster even took another breath, Dempster did a little hop step on one foot and let the other one fly. He snapped Rooster in the jaw so hard, Rooster didn't even blink. He bumped to his knees like he was praying and then he was out.

The principal leaped over and grabbed Dempster by the front of his vest, ripping it apart. He used his huge hands to hold him dangling there.

He leaned into his face and bellowed, "What the Sam Hill you think you're doing? Kicking our second-highest scorer on the chin bone? Are you people, you *gerbils*, trying to kill off my entire ball team? You three are troublemakers—an oddball, an outsider and a savage darky who acts like a homo."

"Hal!" It was Mr. Mylo!

I hoped he'd seen the whole thing.

He walked his quick little step up to the principal.

"Get your hands off that boy, Hal."

The principal did as he was told.

"This isn't the first time you've been unfair to kids who're doing Cot proud. I heard how you treated Cozy in assembly—shame on you!"

Mr. Mylo took a deep breath. I could tell he was just getting started.

"Every opportunity, you favor the dimwits over the bright kids. And you can't keep your mind off the girls long enough to do what you were hired to do. It's been brought to my attention you've been after your very own nieces!"

I looked over at Selda. She was wearing a tiny smile that told me a thing or two about how he came to know that.

Mr. Mylo smoothed the lapels of his suit, composed himself. "As chairman of the Board of Education, it is my duty to tell you you've screwed up for the last time."

"Sorry, Mr. Mylo." The principal towered over Mr. Mylo, but he looked hangdog as any wrongdoing boy. "I'll be better."

Mr. Mylo jammed a natty fedora on his head and said, "Too late, Hal, you've gone the limit. Mayor Lynch sat right next to me tonight. He's making it official Monday: you're fired."

The principal wrung his bullying hands, then turned and fled.

Rooster groaned and opened his chickeny eyes.

Mr. Mylo, Cot's main tycoon, our friend, looked down at him. "Kaminski, you threaten this young lady again"—he nodded at Selda—"you're off any team you're on."

Rooster blinked like he'd wakened in Hades.

Mr. Mylo glanced over at me and winked.

I guess he wasn't about to let his grandmother's accordion get put to shame.

It had been a big night, and it wasn't over yet.

After the show, we had sundaes, and Selda went off wherever it was she needed to go.

Dempster and I took a walk in the breezy woods above Starlight Drive. We snuggled beneath the trees, the black lace of leaves *shush-shush*ing overhead. There, sheltered from the bold-eyed stars, we had at it. At least as far as kissing goes.

CHAPTER 23

Just When Things Get Right

Dempster and I were going steady. I'd glued a little picture of him inside my locket so both of us would be in there. The heart-shaped charm dangled between the silver half note and the silver eye.

Being in love with my best friend put me on top of the world.

He was a more friendly person than I was. I saw that now. More interested in being with other kids, which led to him spending time with girls I'd rather he didn't, and guys, who I didn't mind about. I watched him real close, trying to be in his shoes the way Momma said. I knew that tampering with a good thing like openheartedness would not be loving on my part.

Dempster loved me. And like everything he did, it was one hundred percent.

All the good fortune and all the good feelings inspired me. I'd handed in a ton of extra-credit work that would make my end-of-the-year grades the best ever. And kids who never talked to me before acted like being in the Gerbils made me a celebrity.

Just around the corner was the wedding and a swell new life on Starlight Drive.

Everything was roses.

And then a tragedy befell.

I was headed home from school early. Dempster had gone to Centerville with his mom. Selda had been so broody and unpredictable since getting locked up for a night in Juvenile Detention, I didn't feel like practicing with just her. Besides, we had the wedding tunes down.

I'd taken to using the alley door into the kitchen as my personal entryway. That way, if Dempster and me—I!—took secret late walks while Momma was working up front, she wouldn't exactly know when I left and when I got back.

A block before I reached home, I got the heebie-jeebies, the first in quite a while. I was looking forward to picking up Starch and petting him to calm myself down. Usually he started meowing the second I turned into the alley. This didn't happen, and it spooked me.

"Starch? Starchy-cat?" He had no hearing, but I called him just the same.

Instead, a furious black tomcat shot in front of me, his one eye flashing bad luck.

My mouth went dry and I noticed I was suddenly tiptoeing. The alley had never seemed so long. So dark! And it was just a few minutes after school! Every trash can bulged with tales, and the air was thick with something dreadful.

"Starch?" My voice juddered along with my heart. And then I saw him. "Oh no, Starch, oh no . . ."

He was stretched in front of the back door, his whole body split open and his innards coming out. I was struck dumb, so shocked by the sight I swooned. When I dropped to my knees, the worst thing in the world happened. He opened his eyes and looked at me. A tiny, tiny mew came out of his precious mouth. I screamed for Momma and she came running.

She shouted upstairs, "Help, Artie! Come help us quick!"

When he didn't come, she ran in the kitchen for a dishtowel and wrapped my cat tight inside it. She tried not to jounce him as we ran-walked down two blocks to Dr. Lander's. I was wailing so loud, the doctor came rushing into the waiting room himself.

He peeled back my cat's eyelid and shook his head.

"It's gone, Miss Bettina. Miss Baby Girl. I'm real sorry."

He turned and opened the towel, keeping his back between us and the sight.

Momma was wringing her hands. "Was it that he got run over?"

Dr. Lander was frowning real hard. He took Momma aside and said, "It's been cut stem to stern. That's not from getting hit."

I heard him, and they knew I did.

I cried all the rest of the day.

Stanley closed his shoe store in Centerville early and drove to our shop. After he added up all the facts, he called the law.

Sheriff Brasher came straight over.

There were low words between them, then I heard the sheriff tromp upstairs to Artie's and knock.

We heard Artie protesting, then he banged downstairs and out the back door, we could hear him cursing and kicking cans in the alley.

The sheriff tromped back down and came into our shop. I could imagine him taking off his wide-brimmed hat the way he did, shaking his head.

"When Arthur calms down, he's going t'meet us at the station. I'm telling you now, this is going to take some hashing out. We might as well go on over, start filling out papers."

I heard a few more words between the men, repeating what a sorry business this was, and Stanley saying he needed a couple of minutes to get ready. Finally the sheriff went out to wait in his cruiser.

Stanley made a phone call, then came back to where I was dug into the Murphy. He sat down next to me. On his lap was a plastic bag big as a bucket, full of banana candies. They were my favorite, and something I hadn't had in a tiger's age.

"You know you mean the world to your mother. And I'm going to do my best to be a real dad to you." He patted my arm, trying to get the hang of comforting a daughter.

"I, uh, know a few things about how it was with you and your father . . . I aim to make up for that."

I cried harder.

"Now, now." Pat, pat. "I just telephoned Fawna. You know that calico of hers?" Pat, pat.

I nodded.

"Well, she had kittens. Good ones, from what Fawna says. The playful variety." I was listening real close. "How 'bout Saturday we go pick you out one?"

"Okay." I smiled in spite of myself. Sniffed. "Will you get me a glass of water?"

Momma said, "Knock, knock?" and came in.

We watched Stanley take down a fresh glass, run the tap till it went cold, the way a real parent does.

It felt good in a way, crying without the use of my mirror. Washing away some of the horror of my sweet cat murdered like that. No way he died of curiosity! I would never get over the sight of his poor guts, and him looking to me for help.

Momma tucked me in. "Me and Stanley got to go over to the sheriff's office with him, file a report about your kitty."

"Did Artie do it?"

They looked at each other. Momma said, "Well, honey, we sure hope not."

They were holding hands. I noticed they sat closer to each other than to me.

"Will you be okay here for a little while? By yourself? Or we can bundle you up, take you with us. You just say."

"I'm fine, Momma. Just real sleepy." I was beyond sleepy. I was too bushed to eat a single banana candy.

"Just don't unlock the door, you know that."

"Night, Momma . . . love you."

"Love you, too, Baby Girl."

They tiptoed out like I really was a baby girl safe inside her cradle.

CHAPTER 24

Born Again Special

The minute I heard the front door tinkle and close behind Momma and Stanley, the air clabbered with ghosts and my eyes popped open. It was dusk, the worst time of the day. I tried to go inside myself, find some comfort, but my Sight brought nothing but scary thoughts. What if it really was Artie who had done the killing? How could Momma and Stanley leave me with a maniac loose somewhere? Wouldn't Artie be mad about us calling the sheriff on him? Wouldn't he come for me?

Did I really have nine lives like my dad used to say? Starch didn't have but the one!

Why did it have to be today Dempster was off somewhere?

I dragged the bag of banana candies up on my chest and

tore open a tough plastic corner. I gnawed a piece, trying to sweeten my thoughts: like, would any of Fawna's kittens come in white? Or where could I get a canopy bed like Selda's for my new upstairs bedroom?

I cast through the exciting things Dempster and I had tried out, the taste of his mouth, the gentle cat-pawing way he touched me, how he suffered if I pressed him too close to my stomach.

But I was too far gone. The distracting feelings that one hundred percent came with thoughts of making out, didn't come. My mind was a strong one, and went right back to its miseries, picking on them like scabs. Old agitations lined up like enemy cheerleaders.

What if Momma came home while I was sleeping and looked in my panties drawer and saw the hidden quiz with a D on it? Or found that old note from the landlady? And what did that note say anyway? There's no such thing as ghosts living in envelopes; I should have read it! I swore I'd never sneak again, I'd be a good daughter to Momma and Stanley–

I jerked, thinking I heard a sound in the alleyway. Was that the doorknob *tick-clicking* like a bomb? Or just the clock? I broke into a sweat.

Momma had only been gone about two minutes and I'd already worn myself thin. I tried to think positive, saying over and over how I was still a child with grown-ups to take care of me.

Then my eyes swam inside my eyelids and I was drowning in a sleep deep as ether.

I woke thrashing from no air. It was dark in the kitchen, but somehow I knew it had been no time since Momma and Stanley went out the front door.

A plastic bag was tied over my head! The one that had had banana candies in it; I could smell them where the plastic sealed my nose and mouth. My hands and legs were tied to the Murphy. How could all this have happened while I slept!

A maniac was in the kitchen! My eyes were fogged by plastic and my own breath, but my other senses worked clear as day. Someone watched me as I fought with the only parts of my body not tied down. I didn't even feel pain as my hands and feet beat against the claws of rope. The more I kicked, the tighter they went! I was one hundred percent trapped! I gasped against the tight nasty plastic, and my heart thudded almost out of my chest.

The body I knew was mine turned cold and numb, as though it was someone else's. My mind drifted to the ceiling and looked down at it, already saying goodbye.

I flailed my strong pelvis, thrashed my head in panic. Banana candies flew off the bed and thumped the floor with useless marshmallow fists.

I tried to say, *Artie! Artie, please!* but it was just a muffled animal sound that came through, no more than my cat's last words.

It was like it took forever, and like it took no time at all. My thoughts were pulled inside to a lost future. I saw Dempster as a fine-looking man sitting on a sofa by a fireplace. Next to him was a smart-looking blond woman (me!) that everyone now called B.G. Our heads were filled with education and careers, and our nursery was filled with babies, each one sweet-natured as Jesus.

Only none of this would come to pass.

No! my body said. *I'm still a kid, and kids are not supposed to die! I'm Baby Girl, who spent eleven and one half months in the womb and came out fat, durable and gorgeous. I am meant to be.*

I was going to be killed again, this time with no Momma around to save me.

Then the last bit of air, the precious banana flavored air, was gone. I threw my head back, sucked the plastic into my throat, bucked with final powerful fury. Went slack.

The black of the room went blacker. The last thing I heard was, "That'll fix her wagon."

Then, with a muffled sob, I died.

A million years later my eyes snapped open to the brilliance of celestial lights! Thunder crashed like toppled furniture, announcing my arrival to Kingdom Come! I felt the candy bag in tatters around the edge of my face, its plastic brushing against my eyes. I gasped the bright clean air and babbled thanks to heaven.

A chromed bolt of lightning the exact shape of a toaster arced over my head. Its explosion focused my brain and swiveled my eyes around. I wasn't at the Pearly Gates, I was still tied to my own bed! A mulatto and a walrus were slugging it out in the corner of the room.

Was I in Hades? Where dads were walruses, and daughters helpless fish waiting to be slaughtered?

Dad was somehow horribly alive, horribly ugly, hair and

mustache singed down to Brillo, burn-scars wringing his face into a grinning monster.

He gritted his teeth the way he did when he'd clobber stray dogs, and swung a ham-bone fist at Selda's head. She ducked and it glanced off the side of her skull, storming the air with pastel barrettes.

Her loosened hair made her look electrocuted on one side.

Dad bellowed like a sea lion and charged again. His thick stumpy legs thudded against the floor, shaking the kitchen with powerful weight.

I croaked for Selda to run, *run!* but my words were just little barks inside my dad's roar, our noise eerie as seal-talk.

It didn't matter. She was ready like she's always ready, and smashed him full blast over the head with a chair. He closed his glass-black eyes and sagged to the floor.

Selda said, puffing, but calm as you please, "You breathin', Baby Girl?"

"Yes, thank you."

Each breath I took brought the whiskey stink of my dad into my lungs! A familiar stink, identical to the shattered bottle that nearly murdered Cozy! And no doubt was meant to murder me!

I stared at Dad's broiled-walrus face, snores pushing past the fur trap of his mouth. I didn't look a single thing like him. It was my momma I looked like after all. Except for my special frame.

Selda peeled the rest of the plastic away from my head, yanked at my ropes, finally fumbled through a drawer for the butcher knife. She frowned as she concentrated, sawing at the ropes till her face ran with sweat.

I frowned along with her, hoping my ankles wouldn't get accidentally hacked off—then suddenly I was free! I kicked off the scraps of rope and jacked forward. Sitting up turned me dizzy and sick to the stomach.

Selda riffled her shoulder blades and straightened herself. Except that her yellow eyes bulged a little more than usual, her face stayed right in place. I sighed when she touched her cool hand to my forehead. Closed my eyes.

Which was the worst mistake of my life.

When I opened them again, looked beyond Selda, my dad was no longer passed out on the floor. He was not only up, he was moving fast and silent. He hoisted the hundred-pound meat grinder, something I'd never have thought possible, and swung it over his head. Raring to do what he did best: kill his one and only daughter.

His face was a lunatic mess, his wet-stone eyes even scarier than the web of trailer-burn scars. They shimmied with hate for me and for everything else helpless and small.

He bared his tusky yellow teeth and charged.

There wasn't even time for a warning. I grabbed the knife from Selda and pushed her from between me and the enemy.

I faced him, blade clenched in both hands, ready.

He roared at the sight of it, but could no more halt himself than if he'd been a train. His onrushing belly met the knife. For just that second, time froze, and I believed the world was safe.

Then the knife—huge, scary-looking, dull—bounced heavily off my dad's thick hide, doing nothing but knock me back on the Murphy.

The knife skittered over by the open back door. Selda made a dive for it, hoping for a second try at him.

Dad swayed in place, trembling from holding the meat grinder overhead. He stared down at the ripped spot in his shirt where his stomach should have been stabbed.

What happened next shocked me as much as him.

The velvet curtain swung wide, and in one harmonic bellow Artie and Stanley cried, "Stop!"

Momma took one look at Dad and screamed bloody murder.

Dad swiveled his head to them, blinked once, then dropped the meat grinder onto his own head.

For a second, his neck seemed to disappear into his chest—like something in a Tom and Jerry cartoon—and then his life flew violently out of his body. He crumpled silently to the floor, and it was over.

"Baby Girl!" Momma threw herself across the Murphy, covering me like I was still in danger. "Baby Girl—you all right?" Her voice shook with horror.

I nodded my head. Only the sweet cool spot where Selda touched my forehead kept me from starting in crying.

"What the heck, what the *heck*—" Artie gasped, unable to take in what he'd just seen. "What the—"

Stanley elbowed him in the side. "Shape up."

My eyes peeled away from Dad's ruins. I looked past the tremble of Momma's shoulders, seeking out Selda. Except she wasn't there. Not a trace of her, beyond a cool breeze coming through the back door.

CHAPTER 25

Everything Is Okay

I peeked up past Momma's sheltering arm for a second, watched Stanley's and Artie's neck muscles popping as they hoisted Dad's body and headed back through the curtain with it.

Stanley elbowed the light switch, leaving us in darkness. His calm, low-voiced instructions came to me in broken snatches, ". . . hold him steady, don't knock down the curtain, important thing's . . . umpf! . . . getting him out of here, away from the eyes of the child . . . the sheriff's cruiser still out front?"

In between Artie fretted. "What the heck's gone on here? Who *is* this scar-faced maniac? . . . You think he'd really've heaved that grinder at her? . . . Can't you see the sheriff's car's gone? . . . I can't *believe* you thought I killed that cat . . . I can't even kill the *rat* lives under my bed . . . and you think you wouldn't be a little peevish, *I'd've done to you what you did to me?*"

It was the most I'd ever heard the brothers say to each other, but it was like neither one was listening.

Momma held me so close I was almost smothered. She said over and over, "Now, now, everything's okay, honey, everything's okay."

Finally I was forced to look up and say, "Momma, everything *is* okay."

She nodded and settled down. We just stayed lying there in the dark, our presence a comfort to each other as we tried not to think our thoughts. A siren screamed up the block, then the muffled, excited men-voices filled the front of the shop. Finally they *oof*ed the body out the front door.

Not one of the men came back to bother us.

The smell of spilled banana candies grew overpowering. I knew I'd never eat another one as long as I lived. Which would no doubt be a very long time.

I struggled to keep my mind from going back over what had happened. Instead, I wondered where Selda was right then. If she had yet more streets to tend, more sights to see that night.

Finally, Dempster came to me, in the form of a comforting feeling. Would I be telling him about tonight? Someday? Or would it stay secret? Giving me a dose of womanly mystery . . . My breathing turned deep and even.

The front door slammed, Artie's footsteps skipped upstairs, the siren screamed its way back to the sheriff's office. Carrying my dead father out of our lives forever.

Finally, a velveteen swish as Stanley brushed back through my reading room. The kitchen curtain parted and a wedge of light fell across us, Momma still patting my back for all she was worth.

Stanley leaned over her and whispered real soft, "She's asleep now, Bettina, don't be waking her."

Momma rose quietly to him. Through 'possum eyes, I watched them gaze down at me.

"What were we *thinking* to leave her alone?" she whispered. "I knew the minute we got to the sheriff's we shouldn't—"

"Shhh, shhh, she's fine." He gently led her out of the kitchen.

"But what if . . ."

The curtain fell. Their voices faded, and I wearily turned over on my side and curled around myself. I stared at Aunt Lubmilla's pillow. The yellow-eyed angel, familiar, unblinking, stared back at me.

My past and future lives gathered in the dark, so many of them, I fell asleep counting.

ABOUT THE AUTHOR

SUSANNA VANCE and her husband, sculptor Donald Wright, live in a home nestled in the hills of Astoria, Oregon, overlooking the Columbia River where it meets the Pacific Ocean. She has worked as a teacher, professional photographer and newspaper writer. Her short stories have appeared in several literary publications, and she has been nominated for the prestigious Pushcart Prize. *Sights* is her first novel for young adults.